# THE DAVIS TRIPLETS
# AND THE
# FILM ACTION

# THE DAVIS TRIPLETS

## AND THE

## FILM ACTION

BERNARD PALMER

ANEKO PRESS

Please note that several books in the Danny Orlis series are published by Sword of the Lord Publications and are available for purchase on their website, www.swordbooks.com.



Aneko Press Youth

www.anekopress.com

Aneko Press, Life Sentence Publishing, and our logos are trademarks of Life Sentence Publishing, Inc.
203 E. Birch Street
P.O. Box 652
Abbotsford, WI 54405

**JUVENILE FICTION / Religious / Christian / Action & Adventure**
Paperback ISBN: 979-8-88936-094-0
eBook ISBN: 979-8-88936-095-7
10   9   8   7   6   5   4   3   2   1
Available where books are sold

# CONTENTS

# CHAPTER 1

# LOGGER'S TRAIL

Gary Trumbo, perched precariously on a camera case and a number of boxes of film that had been loaded in where the rear seat of the small plane should have been, moved closer to the window and looked out. Great clouds wrapped themselves about the mountaintops on either side, almost blocking his view of the narrow, writhing band of water below. The plane had been in the air almost three hours. That meant they should be nearing their destination – or so the gangling, fourteen-year-old towhead thought.

"We should be getting close, shouldn't we?" he shouted above the roar of the motor.

Del Davis, who was piloting the heavily loaded float plane, nodded. Del had just earned his aviator's license and was enjoying the feeling of freedom it gave him to fly a plane on his own. The feeling of freedom was increased by the fact that this was the first vacation he had had in a long time. Having decided not to go to college, he had had a full-time job as a mechanic ever since his high school graduation. And after a year of working, he was finally eligible for a vacation! "Another thirty minutes and we should be on the water in front of Logger's Trail," Del said, smiling.

"Sounds great, doesn't it, Ross?"

Ross Kingsley, the other passenger, who was about Gary's age, turned and grinned back at him. The three were headed for the old mining town in British Columbia to help in the production of a missionary film. The mission that carried on its work in that part of the northwest had felt the need to make its operation more widely known. It was decided that a promotional film would be the best way to help people understand the mission and its activities. Danny Orlis, who had long been associated with the mission, had agreed to head up the project. A director and film crew had been hired and had gone ahead to Logger's Trail to get organized. When the boys arrived with the remainder of the supplies, they would be ready to get rolling on the film.

Actually, Ross had not been slated to make the trip to Logger's Trail. Del Davis had come to help Danny Orlis with the flying. Gary Trumbo, who was temporarily living in the Orlis home with the Davis triplets, was along to help with carrying equipment and running errands. At the last minute Danny had decided it would be good to have Gary's friend Ross along, too. "Ross can help Gary lug stuff around, and I think it will be good for him, spiritually," Danny had said. "He needs to be around Christians. Perhaps this experience will give him a desire to know Christ for himself."

And now they were almost at their destination with the first load of supplies. As they drew closer to the isolated village, they reached a broad valley that spread out before them and on either side as far as they could see. The same river, or another just like it, twisted and turned northward on its way to the huge lake near the horizon.

Gary's excitement grew. He leaned forward and touched Ross on the shoulder. "Look straight ahead. That must be Grand Lake!"

The plane was descending now, and Del guided the aircraft closer to the ground as they approached the village. In a few minutes he circled the wide clearing and dipped below the treetops to land on the choppy surface of the lake.

Both boys turned to peer out at the cluster of log cabins and clapboard houses that were scattered over the hillside. Some looked lived in, but others had windows knocked out and doors half off the hinges, silent evidence of the ravages of winter winds after the mine closing depleted the village population. Three men were standing on the dock, waiting for the aircraft to move in.

"Hey, Ross," Gary exclaimed, "it looks as though we're goin' to have company!"

That did not matter to his stubby companion. Ross was looking out over the huge lake.

"I'll bet the fishing is great!"

"You can bet on that," Del answered. "That was the first thing I asked Danny about."

As Del skillfully edged the plane closer to the dock, two of the three men moved out to the end of it and grasped the wing of the aircraft. Without saying anything, they turned the aircraft about and held her firmly until the young pilot and his companions debarked and tied her there. Ross started for shore, but Del called him back.

"Come on, we've got some unloading to do."

"Sure thing." He grinned sheepishly. "I almost forgot."

With the two boys as passengers, there had not been a great deal of space for freight. It only took a few minutes for them to get their gear out of the little cabin and pile it on shore. The aircraft was empty by the time the local missionaries, Cliff and Rene Coleman, came down to greet them.

They introduced themselves, and Rene invited them up to the house for dinner. "I know you must be hungry after your flight," she said.

Cliff picked up a couple of the bags as they started up the hill. Del and the boys did the same.

"You'll be staying in the guesthouse with the rest

of the film crew, Del," the tall, blue-eyed missionary explained, "and we've got a tent for you two. OK?"

"Sounds great," Gary replied.

When they reached the place where the tents had been erected, Cliff stopped at one and set down his suitcase.

"This is yours."

"How about the others?" Ross asked. "Who're they for?"

"They'll house the supplies Danny and Del will be flying in." He spun on his heel to face the young pilot. "That reminds me. You didn't happen to bring along some extra gas, did you?"

"I've got enough to top off the tanks. Why?"

"Gas is in short supply up here right now. It usually comes in loaded on a bobsled in a Cat train caravan in the wintertime, but this year the last Cat train before breakup didn't make it. It went through the ice about eighty miles south of here."

"Danny said you had written him that we should bring in our own gas supply," Del answered, "but he didn't say why."

"Now you know. We've only been able to get one load on a large, twin-engine Canso since breakup," Cliff continued. "That's not even enough to take care of the people who live here."

At the table a few minutes later, Ross asked about how Logger's Trail had been chosen to be the site for the film.

"We've often wondered that," Cliff Coleman responded. "It isn't because we've had such outstanding success – that's for sure."

"I think it's because the work here is typical of work in the north," Rene said. "We came up here and started work in this tattered, run-down village at the site of an abandoned mine. We have had the same problems most northern missionaries have, with the same disappointments and successes."

They went on to say that Logger's Trail had been a sleepy little northern village at the time the mine was opened. Most of the people who lived there were Indians or white fishermen and trappers. The company had built homes for a hundred families and had brought in the people to fill them. In those days the community had been jumping with activity, and there was talk of building a road to open up the entire area. But the good ore had dwindled, and families had begun to move out as the men were laid off. The village fell on hard times.

Two years later the ore was so scant that the mine could not be operated profitably. Doors to the sheds were bolted and locked, and the machinery was left to rust into uselessness.

Closing the mine had been a hard blow to whatever dreams the hangers-on continued to harbor for reclaiming the glory Logger's Trail had once known. Still, not all the outsiders had left. There were some who had fallen in love with the country and the simple, tranquil life of their Indian friends. Others were waiting, hoping against hope that the mine would be reopened.

Both Indians and whites lived in Logger's Trail. Most were very poor. Some were educated; others, especially among the families that had immigrated to Canada from Europe, could scarcely read and write English.

"So, that's the story of Logger's Trail," Cliff concluded.

As soon as they had finished eating, Del announced that he was going to go for a supply of gasoline at a trading depot at some distance from Logger's Trail. He filled the gas tanks of the plane and took off. "I won't try to get back tonight," he said before leaving, "but I can make it before noon tomorrow if this weather holds." He studied the clouds momentarily. "But don't look for me if it gets sticky. We might be in for a little rain and wind."

Ross and Gary did not go directly back to the mission house or their tent after Del took off. Instead they went down the lakeshore to the place where the fishing boats were pulled up on shore. Neither of them had ever seen boats quite like them. They were homemade and all of the same simple design. They had plywood sides and bottoms with oak ribs and an oak transom. They were flat-bottomed scows, broad of beam, and the gunnels were deep enough to hit the average man at the waist. Forty- and fifty-horsepower outboards were bolted to their sterns.

"These babies are big," Ross observed. "I'll bet they'll take a lot of rough water."

"They'll have to," Gary said, "being used on a lake like this."

A little farther on there were some large canoes pulled far up on the beach and turned over. When the boys had finished examining the canoes, they headed for the trading post. They were almost there when two boys about their age came around the corner of the building. They sauntered up, grinning.

Gary recognized them as two of the guys they had seen on the dock when they had landed. They were as tall as Gary, but stockier. They had the ruggedness characteristic of trappers' sons.

"You're the new guys who're staying over at the preacher's, aren't you?" the one called Sid asked.

"Not exactly."

"That's right," Norm Rhinehart put in. "You're staying out in that tent Aren't you afraid to be all alone out there so far from the preacher?"

The color stole up into Ross Kingsley's cheeks. He did not like having people make fun of him. "Lay off, will you?" he retorted.

"He wouldn't be able to help you if a wolf or a bear decided to come around and help itself to whatever was in your tent," Sid Factor continued. "That's all I was thinking about."

Ross turned away deliberately. "Let's go in the store, Gary."

"That's another thing I want to warn you about," Norm said. "You've got to watch your step all the time you're in the trading post, or you'll get in a bushel of trouble."

"What kind of trouble?" Ross demanded.

"Just don't pick up anything if old Jonas is anywhere around. He's got eyes in the back of his head. If you try it, he'll have his mitts on you before you get it in your pocket."

"That's not going to bother us," Gary told him firmly. "We don't do that sort of thing."

Ross Kingsley winced. Gary probably had not ever picked up anything in his whole life, being a missionary's kid and everything. But it was different with him.

"I think he's trying to tell us they're so religious they wouldn't take something that doesn't belong to them," Sid sneered.

"If that's the case we'd better get out of here," his companion said. "We wouldn't want to contaminate them."

They were both laughing as they turned and sauntered away.

# CHAPTER 2

# GRIZZLY TERRITORY!

When the boys returned to the mission house, a bitter wind was whipping in from the north, and it had begun to rain. Clouds whipped over the treetops.

"I'll bet Del won't make it back tonight," Gary observed.

"I talked with him a few minutes ago by radio," Mrs. Coleman said. "He arrived all right, but the weather's bad there, too. He'll stay until it clears."

Ross went over and sat down. "That means we won't have anything to do until tomorrow, at least."

"Or the next day, or the next," Cliff said. "When we get a storm like this, we can usually count on it lasting a few days."

"Maybe we'll get a chance to go fishing before we have to start work," Ross put in hopefully.

Cliff Coleman was right about the weather. The

next two days were duplicates of the first evening at Logger's Trail. The lake was in a fury. Deep-troughed swells piled higher and higher in a foaming, white cascade. They were not ordinary whitecaps, scattered over the big body of water. They ran from wave to wave, continuously, until the entire lake was ridged with white.

Ross and Gary slept in their tent, but Rene insisted that they spend their waking hours in the house.

"There's no use in your sitting out in that cold tent looking at each other," she said.

The morning of the third day was different, however. The sun broke through the clouds and began to chase them away. The wind slacked off, and by noon the lake was placid, as if exhausted by the fierce, restless pounding it had just received.

"Looks as though Del should make it back here this afternoon for sure," Gary said as he and his friend left the house after lunch.

Ross was staring wistfully at the lake. "I sure wish we could go fishing today. If we don't before the rest of the gear and the crew get here, we're not going to be able to."

Gary did not reply. It would not do any good to think about going fishing unless they used a canoe or a boat small enough that they could row. There was not enough gas at Logger's Trail to take care of the commercial fishing boats. They would not be able to get any to use for fun.

They were walking aimlessly around the village when the two boys they had met earlier approached them.

"We stopped by your tent a couple of times," Sid Factor said, "but you weren't around."

"What's the trouble?" Norm put in. "Couldn't you take it?"

Ross flushed. "Would you stay in a tent without heat if you could be in a nice, warm house?"

The burly trapper's son laughed. "If I had my choice of bein' in a tent or where that missionary could preach at me for two days, I'd take the tent. How about you, Sid?"

"I don't know. Maybe they like bein' preached at." He looked from Ross to Gary and back again. "There are guys so stupid, y'know."

"What did you want to see us about?" Ross Kingsley demanded irritably.

"We just came to see if you guys'd like to go fishin' with us, that's all."

Gary was surprised and showed it. "You mean now? This afternoon?"

"Can you think of any better time?"

"What're you going to do, row?" Ross asked.

The strangers both snorted. "Row? You wouldn't catch us rowin'. There's no chance of gettin' any fish that way. We're goin' halfway across the lake."

"But Cliff told us there isn't any gas to use for sport fishing until Jonas gets some more in."

"That's what he says. There are always ways of gettin' around little problems like that, if you know how."

"How about it?" Sid repeated. "Do you want to go fishing with us, or don't you?"

Gary wanted to go out on the lake and try his luck, but he did not like the looks on the boys' faces. They might be kidding, but the way they talked about getting gasoline bothered him.

"No, thank you," he said.

"Now wait a minute, Gary," Ross protested. "Just speak for yourself. You can stay home if you want to, but not me. I'm goin' fishin'."

"That's more like it," Norm cut in. "I'm glad one of you knows how to have fun. We've got plenty of tackle."

Ross turned to his companion. "It won't be any fun unless you go with us, Gary."

Gay hesitated. He really did not like the idea of going fishing. He felt uncomfortable around people like Sid and Norm, but he did not like the idea of leaving Ross alone with them, either.

"Please."

"OK. You've talked me into it."

* * *

Danny arrived at the railhead just before Del took off to return to Logger's Trail. Young Davis waited for Danny to refuel the plane, and they made the trip together, arriving shortly after Ross and Gary returned from their fishing trip. Del had brought back a supply of gasoline.

Some of the men from the village came to help unload the plane. "You want to be careful where you store this," one of the men joked as he helped put the gasoline into the tent next to the one the boys were sleeping in. "We're apt to come back after dark and help ourselves."

When the men had finished helping them unload the two aircraft and put the supplies away, they sauntered back to the Trading Post to sit on the steps. Del turned to Cliff Coleman.

"That guy didn't mean that crack about stealing our gas, did he?"

The missionary shook his head. "There isn't a more honest man in the north than Pete Sauer. Of course, gas is in short supply around here now. I don't think it would be wise to leave it out carelessly, where it would be a temptation to someone."

Since the supplies had arrived and been unloaded, Danny and the cameraman and Arturo, the film director, wanted to start getting down to work on the film. While they did not plan on doing any serious work until the first of the following week, they did start that day to film some of the more simple scenes. The cameraman wanted to get some scenic shots while the clouds and sun were right, and they had to get some stills to use in publicity. Afterward,

Danny and Cliff took Arturo to some of the more interesting places around the lake, looking for possible sites for some of the dramatic filming. Gary and Ross accompanied them.

The boys could see why the mission had chosen the Logger's Trail area as the setting for the film. The big lake, surrounded by trees and with the mountains in the background, was breathtakingly beautiful.

The following morning was Sunday, and Gary and Ross slept in a little later than usual. They were just getting dressed when Sid and Norm stopped by to ask them about going fishing again.

"This is Sunday," Gary explained. At first he thought that would be explanation enough. Then he realized they might not know what difference that would make. "We're going to have services in a little while. Why don't you go with us?"

Surprised by his invitation, they studied his young face with growing contempt. "Go to church?" Norm repeated. "That preacher would fall over in a faint if we showed up."

"That's right," his companion continued. "He might get so shook up he'd have a heart attack or something. You wouldn't want that to happen, would you?"

Gary laughed. "I'd be willing to take a chance."

"We'd better not." They began to leave. "We'll see you tomorrow – if you survive all this religion."

Ross was glad they had indicated they would be coming around again. He had been afraid they might be so turned off by what Gary had said that they would not want to have anything to do with either one of them.

"That sounds great. If we don't have to work tomorrow, we'll go fishin' with you again," Ross said warmly.

"We'll have to see about that," Norm retorted indifferently.

Ross Kingsley watched them saunter away, his uneasiness growing. "You really blew it this time. We'll never get another chance to go fishin' with them again," he grumbled.

Danny and Del had to go to the railhead to pick up the people who would be taking the leading parts in the film, and the director had a few last-minute changes to make in the script. Then Danny flew his plane back to the place where he had rented it. Del went along in his own plane in order to bring Danny back again. While they were gone, there was not very much work for Gary and Ross to do. When Sid and Norm stopped by and asked them to go out on the lake again, Ross jumped at the opportunity.

"You can finish the work alone, can't you?" Ross asked Gary.

"I guess so."

"Leave what you want to, and I'll do it alone as soon as we get back. OK?"

He went off with Sid and Norm, hurrying as though he was afraid Gary would think of some way to stop him if he lingered. When he came back late that afternoon, his young face was flushed with excitement.

"You should've been along!" he exulted. "You should've been with us! Fishing was a lot better this afternoon than it was last time we went out. Come down to the lake with me and take a look at the size of some of those whoppers!"

When the planes returned, Danny took Arturo out on the lake to one of the islands. It was quite a distance from the village, but it was so scenic. It was one of the places they had chosen for quite a bit of the filming. The director was enthusiastic about the interest it would add to the film. Danny liked it too, but for different reasons. There was a good, well-protected place to dock the boats, and a cabin not very far from the water. There would not be a lot of extra work to take equipment over to it.

At first Arturo wanted to start filming right away on the island; but in the morning, when they were to begin work, he changed his mind.

"We'd make better time," he said, "if someone could move some of our gear across to the island while we film here. Then, when everything is over there, we can go and start to work right away."

Gary grinned at Ross. "You know who he's talking about when he says 'somebody can move the gear,' don't you?"

"I've got a good idea," Ross replied.

Del helped the boys load the boat with the items that Arturo and the cameraman would need, and ferried across to the island. The first load was not too valuable – some inexpensive props, one of the small generators, and some canned food. Those things were stored in the sagging, old cabin.

Ross walked around the cabin, looking at it thoughtfully. "Can you imagine anyone living here?"

"It was probably a very nice cabin when it was first built," Del said. "It was a lot bigger than most cabins around here."

Gary had to agree with Ross. But although the cabin was fairly large, it was in an advanced state of disrepair. Windows were broken out, doors sagged on their hinges and the cement that had chinked the cracks between the logs was long since gone. It was hard to believe that it had ever been livable.

They went back to the mainland for another load. This time Arturo insisted that somebody stay with the gear after it arrived at the island.

"We've got some gas, our food supplies, and some other items that would cost a lot of money to replace," he informed them. "We can't take a chance on their being stolen."

"Cliff says the people around here don't steal," Del reminded him.

"That gear is worth so much, and it was quite a job to get it all out here. I wouldn't leave it anywhere without having someone watch it. Do you know what would happen if it were stolen? We'd be done, finished, until we could get more supplies out."

"I'll stay with it," Del volunteered.

"We'll stay with you," Gary added quickly.

Once they were back at the island and had the canned goods and the rest of the equipment safely stored in the cabin, they decided to go out on the lake for an hour or so. When they came back, they had a nice string of fish.

"I'll make you guys a deal," Del said. "I'll fry 'em for supper if you'll fillet them."

"You've got a deal!" was the response.

Gary and Ross cleaned their catch and left the waste on the beach.

"Did you bury the entrails?" Del asked.

The boys shook their heads. "Sid and Norm didn't bury them when they cleaned their fish," Ross replied. "They said there are so many gulls around it would be all cleaned up before morning."

"Maybe so." Del seemed as though he had something more to tell them but changed his mind. "Only I don't think we'd better do that. Let's bury the waste."

"We'll take care of it as soon as we finish eating," Gary told him.

By the time they ate and did the dishes, however, they had completely forgotten that they had left the fish remains unburied on the beach.

Del had Gary get his Bible, and the three were just finishing devotions when they heard a noise outside.

"What's that?" Ross asked quickly.

With that it came again – a low, guttural growl.

Del Davis sat up sharply. "This is grizzly territory!"

# CHAPTER 3

# ISLAND MISADVENTURE

The sound reverberated through the little building. This time it was much closer than before; a deep, ill-tempered grumbling. The boys stared at each other. The color faded from their cheeks, and their very breathing seemed to cease. They squinted narrowly at the patch of green framed by the broken window.

Gary shifted uneasily. "Wh-what is it?" he stammered.

"It–it's a b-bear!"

Gary was not quite ready to accept that. "We're on an island. There wouldn't be any bears way out here!" He read the disagreement in Del's eyes. "Could there be?"

"I'm afraid a bear wouldn't have much difficulty getting out here," Del answered. "I've heard Danny tell about seeing bears in the Lake of the Woods swimming from one island to another, or even from the mainland."

While they listened, another bear approached the cabin. They could hear him lumbering noisily through the bush.

Ross cleared his throat uneasily. "What would bring them around here?"

"They probably smelled the fish waste you guys left on the beach," Del told him. "That'll bring bears if there are any in the area."

"I didn't think they'd come as quick as all that," Gary said. He moved quietly across the rough, board floor until he could look out the window. The sun had set, but it was still light outside, and the entire clearing was visible. "Would you take a look at that baby? He's the biggest bear I ever saw!"

Ross started for the window but paused long enough to question Del. "We're safe in here, aren't we?" he asked. "They wouldn't try to get in here?" The inflection in his voice made a question of what he said.

"They might. You can never tell what grizzlies will do." Del did not want to frighten his younger companions, but he wanted to be prepared in case the bears did come in. He had to find a place the three of them could go to be safe. Grizzlies could climb better than any man, which was true, but they were heavy animals. They had to find some place the bears couldn't reach. "Let's get up among those rafters. That rickety, old door isn't going to hold those guys out very long after they find it."

He did not have to urge Ross and Gary to do as he suggested. They got up on the table and swung themselves up among the rafters. As soon as they were safely located Del did the same. And not an instant too soon. The biggest bear leaned against the door, and it gave way.

"Get your feet up!" Del shouted.

Everything seemed to happen at once. The bears went wild at the smell of food, clawing and tearing at the sacks and cardboard boxes. Flour spilled across the floor, and a gallon jar of honey broke when it was knocked off the little bench in the corner. One of the grizzlies took a swipe at the camera, knocking it across the cabin floor, but fortunately it was protected by a heavy, steel case. The rest of the equipment did not interest the bears. They were only after the food they could smell.

The boys clung to their perches, hunched low against the roof. The scene below was terrifying. Their position would have been precarious enough with black bears on a feeding spree; with grizzlies it was infinitely more dangerous. If one of them jumped on the table and reared, he would easily be able to reach them with his savage claws. They all had heard of cases where grizzlies had actually climbed trees to get at their victims.

Del and Gary prayed silently, asking God to take care of them and Ross and to keep them safe.

But the bears did not seem interested in them.

They were zeroing in on something to eat. For twenty minutes or more, the grizzlies ravaged the cabin, shredding their sleeping bags and eating the last of their food except that in a few small tins. Then, unaccountably, the bears left as suddenly as they had come. Gary breathed a prayer of thanksgiving as they left the cabin, and he heard them rumbling noisily through the brush.

"They're gone!"

"If they only stay away!" Del added.

Ross remained silent for a time, staring numbly at the havoc below. "You don't think they'll come back, do you?"

Del had not had any experience with grizzlies and said so. "But from what I have read or heard about them, they're completely unpredictable. They might come charging back in ten or fifteen minutes, or we may never see them again."

"Then you're not getting me down from here tonight."

However, the bears must have satisfied both their curiosity and their hunger. There was no sign of them for the rest of the night. Still, the boys did not leave the safety of their perches until the morning sun chased the darkness away.

When they heard about it, Danny and Cliff were more disturbed than the boys, who had gone through the ordeal.

"God was really with you guys," Danny told them.

"I hope you realize that. Those grizzlies could have ripped you up as easily as they did your sleeping bags."

He then spoke with Arturo about finding another place to do the filming they had planned for the island.

"If you think it's best," the director agreed. "This place is ideal, but it's not worth the risk of having someone killed or seriously hurt."

Cliff Coleman did not agree with him, though. He had been living in the area for several years and knew the ways of the grizzlies.

"I don't think leaving here would solve the problem," he replied. "There are grizzlies everywhere around here. And they move around so much and so far that I don't think it would help us much to move. There's just about as much chance of running into them on one of the other islands or someplace on the mainland as there is here."

Danny was willing to accept his decision. "What would you advise?"

He thought for a moment.

"I think I'd suggest staying away from here for a few days after making sure that everything is cleaned up and buried deep enough so they won't smell it. That would give those bruisers a little time to settle down. Then, when we come back, I'd be real careful not to leave any garbage around to attract them."

Under the direction of Danny and the resident missionary, they all cleaned up the cabin, even scrubbing the floor. They buried everything that had been ruined but not eaten, including the waste from the fish they had caught the night before. Finally, Cliff was satisfied that they had done all the cleaning they could.

"We'd just as well move on," he said. "There's nothing else we can do here."

When they returned to the village, shortly before noon, Sid and Norm were waiting for them. They called Ross off to one side as soon as he got off the boat.

"We'd sure like to go fishing again," Sid began. He spoke hesitantly, as if there was something that held him back.

"So would I," Ross replied. "The last time we went out was really great!"

"Only there's one small problem." Norm lowered his voice to a whisper.

"Yeah. We got no gas," added Sid. "Nobody will sell us any. They say a fishing trip isn't important enough to waste gas on."

Ross did not know why they were talking to him about that. He did not have any gas, either.

"We'd row out, but that's a waste of time. There's no use in trying to fish anywhere close. We've got to get to one of the good spots if we're going to catch any fish."

Norm looked about to be sure no one else was close. "That's why we came to you. We thought maybe you would help us with a little gas."

"Me?" Ross echoed. "I don't have any gas."

"Now, don't give us that. There's plenty in one of those tents. You could get some if you wanted to."

At first Ross could not be sure he had heard them correctly. Surely they would not ask him to steal – and especially from Danny Orlis and the men who were making the film. They were only giving him a rough time, he decided – trying him out to see what sort of a guy he was.

But that was not what their faces said. They had really meant it when they had asked him to get them some gas.

"But I couldn't do that!" he exclaimed, his manner reflecting the shock that swept over him. "That would be stealing!"

"You don't say!"

"Whatever gave you the idea we'd ask you to do a terrible thing like steal gas?" Sid wanted to know.

"Taking a little gas from one of their barrels wouldn't be stealing. They'd never miss it," Norm said.

Ross did not answer immediately. It was not going to do them any good to urge him to get mixed up in anything like that. He had already decided as much. But how was he going to tell them? If he was not careful, they would get the idea he was some kind of a religious fanatic, the same as Gary. And if that happened, they would be done with him. They would not want to take him fishing or do anything else with him.

"Now, if you happened to be as weird as your buddy,

we wouldn't waste our time talkin' to you," Norm went on. "In fact, we wouldn't be having anything to do with you, period. He's so religious he about drives us up the wall."

Ross did not like it when they criticized Gary. There were a lot of things about his pal that bothered him, but that did not give them any right to make fun of him.

"Cool it," Ross retorted tautly. "He's my best friend."

"We won't hold that against you."

"You'll get the gas for us, won't you, Ross?" Sid pleaded. "All we need is five gallons so we can go fishing."

"It really isn't stealing," Norm persisted. "You're helping them for free. They *owe* it to you."

"Besides, if they decided they wanted to go out and get some fish, you wouldn't see them staying in. It wouldn't be any different for you to use some to go fishing. It's exactly the same thing."

Ross did not reply. The way they explained it, it sounded reasonable enough. He would only be doing what Danny and the older guys would do if they felt like fishing. It really was almost the same. And he did deserve some kind of pay for all the work he had been doing.

"How about it?" Sid asked.

A couple of men approached them on the path, sauntering up from the water's edge where they had been mending their nets. Norm and Sid fell silent until the men were out of hearing.

Ross waited so long before saying anything that their tempers ignited.

"Are you going to help us out or aren't you? We haven't got a week to fool around while you're making up your mind."

Ross moved some distance away from the path so there would be little chance for him to be overheard.

"I can't risk it, guys!" he explained. "I'd be in a real jam if I got caught!"

"We don't figure on gettin' caught."

"You don't understand. That Orlis character watches me all the time. If I make one wrong move, that's it for me."

With that he told them about shoplifting in Rock Point the year before and being placed on probation.

"If I stole as much as half a gallon of gas and Danny found out about it, I'd be headed for the county home."

What he told them about being arrested earlier was true. It was also true that he was on probation. He had not intended to tell them about his past, but he could not have them thinking he was chicken.

But Norm and Sid responded as though they were his best friends. "Old Jonas has caught us snitching cigarettes and candy and hunting knives from the Trading Post," Sid confided. "Every time it happens he says he's goin' to call the RCMP, only he never does. He just yells at us."

# CHAPTER 4

# NIGHT OF EXCITEMENT

Ross was deeply troubled by his conversation with Sid and Norm the rest of the day, in spite of the fact that they did not approach him again. He could not understand why they had singled him out. They did not know anything about him.

They made fun of Gary for being such a religious fanatic, but they did not ask him to help them steal gas. And even when they made fun of his pal, there was a certain respect in their attitude – a respect they did not have for him. He found that disturbing.

Well, he told himself firmly, they would find out that he was no different than Gary when it came to stealing, if they did not know already. That was one thing he was not going to do again, no matter how much they pressured him.

Ross thought about mentioning his conversation with Sid and Norm to Gary, but decided against it.

He knew what Gary would start talking about. He would begin to tell him about Jesus Christ, as though Christ would solve his problem. "If you confess your sin and put your trust in Christ, He'll give you a new life," Gary would say. "If that happens, Sid and Norm will soon know that you're different than they are, and they won't bother you anymore."

Ross had had enough of Gary's preaching to last him a long time. He was not going to deliberately give him an opportunity to start again.

That night Ross and Gary went to bed at the usual time, crawling into the bedrolls that Rene Coleman had improvised for them to take the place of the sleeping bags the grizzlies had tom up. They were just about asleep when they heard muffled sounds coming from the next tent. Gary Trumbo opened his eyes abruptly and sat up.

"Ross!" he cried in hushed tones. "Ross! Are you awake?"

"What's the matter?"

"I heard somebody in the storage tent."

"But why would anybody be out there?"

And then Gary remembered – that was where their gas was stored! His eyes widened and his lips parted slightly. He leaned forward, straining to pick up any strange sounds from beyond the canvas walls of their tent. He knew Ross was sitting up, even though he was not looking in his direction.

"There's somebody out there!" Gary croaked.

"Somebody's stealing our supplies – maybe our gasoline!"

"That can't be!"

The only ones Ross could think of who would do a thing like that were Sid and Norm. After he turned them down when they asked him to steal some gas for them, they just might have decided to get some gas on their own. They were daring enough to do a thing like that if they wanted it badly enough. If they had not been lying when they were bragging to him, they had stolen plenty of stuff and would not hesitate to steal the gas in the tent if they thought they had a fair chance of getting away with it.

Ross inhaled a deep breath and expelled the air thoughtfully. He did not trust his new friends, but surely they were too smart to steal gas themselves after he had turned them down. They would know that Ross would be on to them right from the start. All he would have to do would be to tell Danny and Cliff Coleman, and they would both be in real trouble.

Of course it could be that they were counting on the fact that he was such a good friend he would not squeal on them, even if he did know they were guilty. That thought warmed him.

Then he realized there could be another reason why they were so bold. They knew he had been in trouble with the law. They just might figure he was the same as they were and would not give them away.

Now that he thought about it, he was sure that was closer to the truth.

Of course, he was only guessing that it was Sid and Norm stealing the gas. It could be anybody. Practically every person in the village needed gas badly enough to consider stealing it. And there were those who did not live in the village, who made their homes out in the bush, who could have come in to steal their fuel.

The sound came a third time, disturbing the hush of night. There was the harsh, metallic clang of metal against metal.

"Somebody's out there!" Gary shrilled, scrambling out of his bedroll and into his trousers.

Ross was sitting up but made no attempt to join his companion in getting dressed.

"It–it's probably just a dog," he stammered.

"No dog ever made *that* noise!" Gary groped for the flashlight in the murky darkness of the tent. "Get your clothes on! We've got to see what's going on out there!"

Ross obeyed reluctantly. "OK. OK, but I still don't think there's anything wrong. Not every noise is made by thieves."

Gary did not say any more, but he could not understand why his pal was so insistent that there was nothing wrong. Even old Whittier in the church back in Rock Point, who was as deaf as a tree, would have heard that noise and would have known what it meant.

Gary would not have been surprised if even Danny and the Colemans had heard that cymbal-like clatter all the way up to the house. It sounded as if somebody carrying a large can or a heavy piece of metal had stumbled against one of the gasoline barrels. He crept out of the tent and switched on his flashlight, sweeping the other tent with its narrow white beam. Ross was directly behind him.

"See!" Ross exclaimed, relief evident in his voice. "What did I tell you? There's nobody around here but you and me!"

"I'm sure there was somebody, though," replied Gary. "Whoever it was must've gotten scared when he banged into that barrel and made so much noise." He crept toward the supply tent.

Ross followed, hesitantly. He hoped Sid and Norm – if they had been the ones making that noise – had been smart enough to get out of there fast. He did not want to see them get in trouble. And he especially did not want to be the one who helped catch them.

When they reached the tent there was no sign of anyone. The boys stopped and looked about, hesitantly.

"Now will you believe me?" Ross asked.

Gary did not reply at once. He knelt and studied the canvas carefully. "I know this flap was tied shut," he said. "I did it myself." He squirmed around until he could look up at his companion. "You should remember that, Ross. You were here with me just before we went to bed."

"I guess you're right," Ross admitted uneasily, "but whoever was here has beat it. There's no one around now!"

"We should have gotten over here a little quicker. Maybe we could've caught the thief." He rose to his feet and stepped into the tent, searching the interior with his flashlight.

"But we can't be blamed. We couldn't be sure anyone was here until that barrel made so much noise. By the time we could get here, whoever it was had had plenty of time to run away."

"I wasn't blaming anybody," Gary said quickly. He paused and examined the barrels. "I don't believe any gas was stolen, though. We can be thankful for that."

After an instant or two Ross shivered and turned toward the opening in the front of the tent. "Let's go."

"Go where?"

"Back to our bedrolls before we freeze to death."

Gary did not know whether they should leave or not. He was cold, too, but that gasoline was important. They did not dare leave it without somebody being awake to guard it.

"Are you going to stay here all night?" Ross demanded.

"I don't think we should leave, at least for a while," Gary said. "Whoever tried to steal our gas just might come back. And if they do, we should be here to nab 'em."

Ross felt sure the thieves would not be back anymore that night and said so. "I know what I'm talking about," he said confidently.

Gary understood. After all, Ross had been in that kind of trouble himself. He knew how a guy's mind worked when he was stealing something.

"I suppose you're right," he acknowledged, "but I still don't want to take any chances."

"We wouldn't be taking a chance," Ross persisted. "Besides, we heard the noise from our tent the first time, and we weren't expecting to hear anything. If someone should be stupid enough to come back after making all that clatter, we'd be sure to hear him if we're listening for him."

Still, the other boy was not to be persuaded to leave, at least for a while. "You go on back to the tent, Ross," he said. "I think I'll hang around here for an hour or so."

"Oh no. I'm not going to leave if you don't."

Gary moved to one side and leaned against one of the barrels. He did not say so, but he was glad Ross was going to be with him. He did not like the idea of spending much time in that tent alone – especially after there had already been one attempt to steal their gas.

For an hour or more they huddled in the tent, shivering, in the night wind blowing off the lake.

Twice Ross got to his feet and moved about, waving his arms to keep warm.

"Do–do you really think it's necessary for us to stay right here in this tent all night?" he asked, his teeth chattering. "We would hear anyone who tried to steal anything."

"Maybe we would and maybe we wouldn't," Gary answered.

"We did a little while ago. We heard them as plain as could be."

Gary had to agree that what his pal said was true. They had heard the noise in the storage tent when they had both been sleeping. Besides, now that the intruder had been frightened away, he probably would not come back. As Ross said, coming back after almost getting caught the first time just did not make sense. And it would be a lot warmer to snuggle in their bedrolls than to sit in an unheated tent.

"Well," he began, "I guess we wouldn't have to go to sleep. We could lie in our bedrolls and at least be warmer than we are now."

"Now you're making sense. Come on before we freeze to death."

Once in the warmth of their bedrolls, however, they became far sleepier than they had been in the storage tent. Gary stirred and called out to his companion. Ross did not answer him.

"Are you awake?" he demanded loudly.

Ross Kingsley muttered something unintelligible.

Gary tried once more to wake him, but when he could not succeed, he stopped trying. It really did not matter whether Ross stayed awake or not, he reasoned, as long as he could do so. That would not be too easy, but he thought he could. But in spite of his good intentions, sleep overcame him.

The next thing he knew, the entire area was ablaze with light. People were running everywhere, shouting excitedly.

"Ross!" he cried.

"What's the matter?" For a brief instant Ross thought someone must have come back to try to steal gas again.

Gary jumped up and went to the flap of their tent and stared outside. The shed behind the Trading Post was aflame, and it seemed that the whole village was awake.

"There's a fire!" Gary shouted. "That shed behind the store is on fire!"

Ross scrambled out of his blankets. "That's where old Jonas keeps his gasoline supply!"

# CHAPTER 5

# COPING WITH THE SHORTAGE

The people were panicky and noisy at first, but when the first shock had worn off, they seemed subdued by what was happening. They stood in a ragged semicircle just beyond the searing, invisible wall of heat. They were awed to silence by the growing frenzy of the fire.

The flames continued to build. As each gas barrel exploded, a column of fire shot high against the dark background of forest surrounding the village. The garish yellow light illuminated every tree, every scraggly bush in harsh detail. The paint on the back of the old store building bubbled and blistered in the sudden heat.

"Get some water on the store, or we'll lose it, too," an Indian cried suddenly.

The spectators were eager for something to do – anything, however small, that would strike a blow at the enemy that was consuming their precious stores of gasoline. They sprang to work eagerly. Magically, buckets appeared, snatched from the nearest cabins and pressed into service.

The men were the first to go to work, but the women and even the children soon joined them, forming bucket lines to move the precious water up from the lake to the back of the threatened building. Men at the end of the line dashed forward, braving the heat, to douse the back of the store with water in a desperate, back-breaking effort to keep it cool enough so it would not burst into flames.

The long line of people worked without letup, passing the buckets from the water's edge in a never-ending stream, only to relay them back to be filled again once they were emptied. Gary and Ross took their places in the line, working mechanically like everyone else, taking a bucket, passing it to the person ahead, and turning to get another and another and another.

It was not long before Ross and Gary were almost exhausted. Sweat soaked their clothes, and air came by gasps into their heaving lungs. Still, they dared not slacken the energy-consuming pace.

Minutes raced by. No one was sure just when it happened, but the fire at last began to lessen in intensity. The flames protested angrily but the fury was gone out of their efforts. The encircling bands of heat crept closer to the shed, shrinking back from the store building.

It was not long until it was apparent that the Trading Post was no longer in danger. Only then did the people stop to rest. They sank to the ground for a time or walked numbly about, trying to shake the fatigue that overwhelmed them. Ross and Gary did not even know that Danny, Del, and Cliff were at the fire until everyone stopped working. As soon as he saw them, Gary went over and told them about the intruders earlier in the night.

"Of course, we didn't actually see anybody," Ross put in.

"But we heard them," Gary protested.

"I'm not surprised," Danny said. "It's obvious to me that somebody started this fire. It's probably the same guys who tried to steal our gas."

"Do you think it was set purposely?" Ross asked, almost defensively.

"The thieves may have dropped a cigarette or caused a spark that ignited it. It doesn't take much to start a gasoline fire."

One by one the villagers straggled back to their homes. Gary and Ross went wearily back to their tent. Cliff turned to Danny and Del. "Let's go up to the house and get Rene to fix us something to eat."

"At three-thirty in the morning?" Danny laughed.

"We're all about starved. Besides, who can sleep after all this excitement?"

At the kitchen table the conversation turned to the problems caused by the fire. The muscles about Danny's mouth tightened. From his boyhood on the Angle, he knew what shortages like this could mean in a place of isolation. It would make things plenty rough for everybody.

Early the following morning Danny and Cliff went over to see the Indian chief and Jonas. The old trader had already been on the radio trying to get an aircraft to bring in a load of gasoline.

"If we could get a Canso load, we'd be able to get by until we have time enough to work out something. But they can't get anything up to us for a week or two." A great weariness seized him. "If they can come then. I couldn't get a promise from them."

Cliff told Jonas and the chief of the Indians in the village that the film crew had some gasoline they were willing to share, as long as it lasted.

"And I think we can fly in enough to keep things going until the Canso can get in here with a big load," Danny said.

Jonas and the Indian chief were grateful but wary. They had had experience with the offers of others in the past, and they knew that usually there were strings attached to every proposal.

"How much will you charge?" the chief wanted to know.

"What the gas costs us, plus the fuel and maintenance on the aircraft for the time we're flying. That would amount to $15.00 an hour for the time we're in the air."

This seemed reasonable to the two men, and the arrangement was accepted.

Once the price for flying in the gasoline was decided upon, Danny told the others about the deal. Del left right away to pick up a supply. He was back late in the afternoon with the first load of gas. As the mission plane came in, the village men stopped what they were doing and hurried down to the dock to unload the fuel. Danny was there, too. He took over the job of refueling and checking out the aircraft while Del had something to eat.

Del flew out to the railhead again that night and was able to bring in another load of gasoline the next morning. Then Danny took his turn and ferried in two toads of fuel. The stockpile was pitifully small, but there was enough to allow each fisherman to buy a certain amount. They lifted their nets and moved them closer to the shore so they would not have so far to go to work them every day. The fishing was not quite as good at the new locations, but at least they were able to get out and lift their nets regularly to keep the supply of fish coming in.

The film crew had shared their town supply of gasoline with those who lived permanently by the lake and had used only enough themselves to keep their work going. Some days they did not use any.

On other occasions they managed to get by with

a few gallons expended in operating the generators to furnish more light.

Danny and Cliff consulted with the villagers daily. They were about to fly in another few loads of gasoline, and then a Canso carrying nothing except fuel came winging in unexpectedly to relieve the situation.

"And I'll be back again the first of the week with another load," the pilot said.

Now that the critical phase of the fuel shortage had eased, the film crew took back a portion of the gas the mission plane had hauled in.

"Now we're really going to work," Arturo told the crew and cast. "We've got to make up for the time we've lost."

"Jonas has hired someone to watch his gas supply," Gary observed. "What about ours?"

Ross volunteered himself and Gary to guard the gas tent, at night, but Danny insisted he would take care of it.

When the boys went to bed in their tent that night, Danny and the missionary were sitting near their supply tent, warming their hands over a small fire. When the boys rose the next morning, however, both men were gone.

"They must've gotten sleepy," Ross observed. "At least we'd have stayed on the job."

On their way to the mission house for breakfast, Gary opened the flap of the supply tent and looked in. The drums were there and the boys were about to go on, when Gary turned back and kicked one. It rang out, hollow as a bell.

"That's strange!"

He kicked another and another, achieving the same empty sound.

"Listen to that!" he exclaimed. "The gas is gone! Somebody stole it!"

Ross moved forward numbly and kicked one of the drums himself. The barrels were empty! And he and Gary had not heard a thing!

"I can't believe it," he muttered.

"We'd better go tell Danny!"

Then men were sitting at the breakfast table with Cliff and Rene Coleman when the boys burst in. Danny must have seen them come up on the back porch. He had stopped eating and was watching them. "Now, what's wrong with you guys?"

"Somebody made off with our gas!" Gary cried. Danny set his coffee cup on the table, deliberately. "Did you look close?"

"We didn't have to look!" Gary exploded. "We kicked the barrels, and they're empty!"

"Maybe you'd better go out and kick them again," Del put in.

"Aw, lay off, will you?" Ross said. "We're trying to be serious."

"Yeh." Gary came to realize, slowly, that they were not concerned about their fuel supply. "You guys moved it yourselves, didn't you?"

"And it's a good thing we did," Cliff said, smiling. "You guys were sleeping so soundly we could have pulled in with a freight train and gotten it. You wouldn't have heard a thing! "

"We weren't *that* zonked out!"

"Actually," Danny explained, "we've been moving the gas out of the tent a little at a time ever since we put it there. Yesterday afternoon we got the last of it."

The boys tried to find out where the gasoline was stored now, but no one would tell them. When they left the breakfast table they still did not know where the gas was, or if all of it had been used.

Not long afterwards, they were out in the yard of the mission house when Sid and Norm came swaggering up. Ignoring Gary, they directed their attention to Ross.

"We hear the RCMP are coming in to find out who set that fire," Norm said.

Ross shuddered inwardly. Ever since he had had that trouble with the police back home, it bothered him to know that they were going to be around. "You couldn't prove it by me."

The four boys started down the slope in the direction of the trading post.

"It isn't that big a deal," Sid said casually. "But it doesn't make any difference to us whether they come or not." He paused for a moment. "How about you, Ross? How does it grab you to have the cops nosing around?"

Ross Kingsley felt the color climb into his cheeks. The thinly veiled accusation in his friend's voice bothered him.

For the next several days, the weather was obstinate. A great, unbroken canopy of clouds hung from horizon to horizon just above the trees, and a chill, wet wind swept in from the lake. It drove the cold into the cabins and stopped work on the film.

Arturo was beginning to become concerned.

"I don't know what we're going to do if we don't get a break in the weather soon, Danny," he said the morning of the sixth day without the sun. "When we started, I thought we'd have the shooting done by this time."

Danny knew about the weather in the north and had warned Arturo about planning their schedule too tightly. Cliff and Rene had also mentioned that there might have to be a delay.

"I told you we could have a stretch of bad weather while we were here and that we should allow for it," Danny reminded him.

"That's true enough," the director said. "Only we didn't have any idea that it would last so long. We've got so much shooting yet to do that I'm beginning to wonder if we're going to be able to finish. We've got another project that has to start the first of next month. It's beginning to worry me."

# CHAPTER 6

# MOUNTIES COME TO LOGGER'S TRAIL

The weather was more perverse this July than anyone could remember it ever having been. Clouds hung low over the forest, blotting out the sun and lengthening the night until it seemed almost like winter, except for the lack of snow and ice. The wind relaxed occasionally, resting from its fury just long enough to allow the white foam to disappear from the breakers. For a few hours it would seem that the bad weather was about to break. Then the wind would gather strength once more and howl across the large mossy bog areas that the Indians called *muskeg* and across the vast stretches of water.

The tension among the men on the film crew built with each passing day of inactivity. Even those who were only indirectly involved began to feel it – especially Danny, Del, Gary, and Ross. But there seemed to be nothing that could be done to change the situation.

"We've had to leave a lot of outdoor scenes until the last because we didn't have enough gasoline to get out on the lake where we would be shooting them," Arturo said. "Now we're ready to film this outdoor stuff, and we can't do it because of the clouds."

Danny tried to encourage him. "A change is long overdue. Weather like this can't last forever."

"I know it's going to change," the director retorted, "but when? We have to be in Indonesia the first of the month. The date's been set for more than a year. People who are going to be involved in it are coming from all over the islands. The script is ready, and we have to start shooting on time."

"What if we don't finish here?" Danny asked uneasily.

"I've explained all this to your mission board," Arturo told him. "They understand that I have a firm commitment in Indonesia that can't be broken."

Half a film, Danny realized, was as good as no film at all. And it might not be possible to come back at another time and finish it. The seasons changed dramatically that far north. And according to the script the entire story of the film took place in the summer. Any delay would have to be a whole year.

Before they separated that evening, Danny and Cliff guided the group in a period of prayer. Everyone in the little mission living room took his turn asking

God to help them out of their difficulties. But Ross could not pray. He had bowed his head, intending to pray, but the words refused to come out.

"A lot of good that praying will do," he blurted when they had finished. "It's just a waste of time."

If he had expected an argument, he was disappointed. No one challenged him.

Two days after they had started praying earnestly for sunshine, the clouds began to lift. There was only a narrow rift in the unbroken shroud at first, but during the morning the clouds began dispersing, and the first rays of sunlight were beginning to peep through.

Ross learned from the director that they would not be filming at least until noon. He went down to the lakeshore where he saw Sid and Norm cleaning out their boat. He was offering to help them when an RCMP aircraft came winging in. It circled the village and touched down on the bay.

Sid stopped what he was doing and watched as the police plane edged skillfully towards the dock. "I thought they'd given up on that fire," the boy murmured. "Why do you suppose they're coming here now?"

"They've got to have something to do to keep them busy," Norm retorted.

Ross Kingsley did not enter into the conversation, but he knew one thing for sure. If he had had anything to do with that fire, he would be mighty uneasy right now.

For some reason, Sid and Norm did not seem as cheerful as they had earlier. They quit working before long and said they were going back into the bush. "You can come along if you want to, Ross."

He really wanted to go with them, but the clouds were continuing to move. Great, fleecy chunks were tom off of the motionless sea of gray, exposing ever widening currents of sparkling blue.

"I'd like to, but it looks as if we'll be able to start shooting again this afternoon," he said.

By noon, the clouds had disappeared, driven beyond the horizon. Excitement gripped the film crew. "It looks as if we're finally going to get rolling again!" one of the actors said.

Del, Gary, and Ross helped the film crew load the boats, and they were ready to leave for the island when the director appeared on the dock. Until that moment he had been up at the mission house checking last-minute changes in the script. The instant Gary saw him he knew something was wrong.

"Cliff's sick," Arturo said. "We're not going to be able to film today, after all."

Even though there were scenes that did not involve the missionary, the director decided against shooting them that afternoon. "We'll want him to approve what we do with all the scenes," he explained.

Ross was glad that Sid and Norm had gone off

without him. It was not so much fun being with them when all they could talk about was the RCMP and the investigation of the fire. In a way he was almost as disturbed as Sid and Norm were by the presence of the officers in the village. He could not see that there was any way that they would link him with the fire, but as long as the police were around, there was always that chance.

He hoped he would not be questioned by the Mounties, and he had his wish. They did not come around to talk with either Gary or him. At first, they asked few questions of anyone they saw, but spent a great deal of time going over the charred remains of the fire. They gave surprising attention to detail. They sifted the ashes carefully, and every now and then they put something in a box they had with them. If anyone hung around too long while they were working, the sergeant in charge politely asked them to find someplace else to loiter. And the first night after they arrived, the site of the fire was roped off and guards patrolled it to keep anyone from disturbing it or removing anything.

Once they had finished with the site itself, they began to ask questions. They interrogated first one after another – politely, but with an insistence that would tolerate nothing less than the complete truth.

There were rumors everywhere. One story was that the Mounties had found the fingerprints of the one who had set the fire. They were going to fingerprint everyone in the village until they found the right prints. Another rumor whispered that they had radioed for a lie detector. As soon as the machine arrived, they were going to call the men and boys in, one by one, and question them until they located the ones who were lying. Still a third story claimed that the RCMP already had discovered who was guilty of causing the fire. All they were waiting for to make the arrests was enough evidence for a conviction.

Actually, though, nobody had any reliable information. The Mounties asked plenty of questions but answered none, and if they had any suspicions, they kept them to themselves.

Everyone was so excited about the presence of the officers in the village that making the film was shoved aside as a topic of interest and conversation.

When the village woke up one morning and was rubbing the sleep from its eyes, the officers were already loading their gear into their plane. Old Jonas had gone down to see them off.

"When are you going to arrest somebody?" the old trader demanded plaintively.

The officers were not angered, but Jonas was unable to persuade them to reveal anything. When the aircraft left, not even the gray-haired trader had any inkling of the success or failure of the investigation.

Gary and Ross were just getting up, as was half the rest of the village, when the plane took off. The boys crouched in the opening of their tent and watched until the plane lifted off the water and swept back over the village in a wide semicircle to head back to its home station.

"Well, they're gone," Ross sighed, revealing his relief.

"Yeah, they're gone." Gary paused, thoughtfully, and took a deep breath. "And they didn't arrest anyone."

Some of the people in the village were critical of the officers because they had left without making an arrest. "All they do," one of the older men told Jonas, "is come in here, poke around in the ashes, ask a few questions and leave. That's the last we'll ever see of them until the next time something happens. If you ask me, I don't think they even care if they find out who caused that fire."

* * *

The weather seemed ashamed of itself for causing so much trouble with the filming the last two weeks or so. Clouds were banished from the sky, except for a few great, billowing shapes that drifted aimlessly about but were considerate enough not to block the sun for more than a few moments at a time.

The missionary still was not feeling well, but he was able to take his part, as usual. Everything was moving along at a brisk pace. They were able to shoot a number of scenes each day. The director took advantage of the change in weather and set up a punishing schedule. While he was working with the cameraman and characters in one scene, Danny would be setting up the next.

Danny Orlis did not know much about making films, but he had helped enough since they had started work at Logger's Trail to have some idea of what was to be done. Arturo was able to correct Danny's errors in a few minutes, moving the camera for a little better angle or shooting against a slightly different background.

Gary, Ross, and Del had to be up and ready to go to work at six each morning. The cameraman and sound man were always there early as well, and they worked long hours in an effort to squeeze everything into the last days of filming.

Arturo hit hard, filming one scene after another, with as little wasted time as possible. By Saturday morning they were finished with one of the last remaining dramatic sequences and were ready to move to a new location.

"The lake's beautiful today," Arturo exclaimed, looking out over the wind-roughed water. "Absolutely beautiful. I think we'll take those boats out and get some shots now."

Danny checked the outboard motors. "We're going to have to get some more gas before we do."

"Maybe we should have the boys check what there is left," Arturo said. "Everything is going so well we can't have a hitch now. If we need more gas, we should send Del down for it tomorrow."

Danny called Ross and Gary over and told them he wanted them to go for the gas. "And be sure to check to see how much we have left over there."

Gary grinned. "Want us to kick the barrels?" he asked.

"No, I don't want you to kick the barrels. I want you to take the cap off and shine your flashlight inside to see how much gas we've got left."

"Now all you've got to do is tell us where to go and we'll be on our way," Ross said.

"I thought you'd guessed. We hid it on the island."

"The island?" Ross echoed. "Out with the grizzlies?"

"They don't drink gas."

"That's about the only thing they don't bother."

"To tell you the truth," Cliff put in, "they're guarding it for us."

"You're not going to get me to go back out there – gas or no gas," said Ross emphatically.

"We won't be there long enough for the bears to bother us," Gary assured him. "We'll go ashore, fill our cans and be on our way before they have a clue we're around."

"Wanna bet?" Ross asked nervously.

# CHAPTER 7

# FORCED LANDING

**R**oss was still protesting going out to the island. In spite of his arguments, however, he climbed into the big, flat-bottomed boat with Gary.

"I want to make it plain to you that I'm not going because I want to. So when the bears eat me up and you have to go back and tell my Mom I was an ugly grizzly's supper, you'll have to say it was your fault."

"I'll try to remember that," Gary said, grinning.

When they reached the island, Ross looked around uneasily as he and his pal pulled their boat up on shore near the place where Danny and Cliff had hidden the gas. He half expected to catch sight of a patch of brown fur or feel his nose pinch with the rank bear smell that lingered wherever the dangerous animals went.

But there was nothing. The boys went ashore hurriedly, checked the barrels, and wrote down how much gas they would estimate to be in each one. Then they headed back to the village with three five-gallon cans of gasoline on the floor of the boat. They covered the cans with an old tarp.

Danny had directed them to use the small dock almost directly in front of the place where they were going to be filming. There would not be as much chance of people seeing the cans of gasoline as if they used the government dock.

Danny had not thought about Sid and Norm, however. They saw the mission boat coming in when it was a mile offshore, and they knew Gary and Ross were in it. When the boys nosed into the dock, the other two were waiting for them.

"You must've been on an errand," Norm said. He was talking to Gary, but his gaze drifted to the tarp-covered gas cans in the bow. "You didn't stay long enough to do any fishing."

Gary slipped the bow line over a dock post and got out without answering. "Ross," he said, "go up and tell Danny that we're ready as soon as they are."

By the time Ross came back with Arturo and the others, the local pair was gone.

"Think they saw our gas?" he asked when he and Gary were alone.

"Norm was really staring at it. I'm sure he guessed what we have in here."

That evening, the boys told Danny how much gas was still stored on the island. He and Arturo decided it would be best for Del to fly out for another load. Since the next day was Sunday, Danny asked Del to be ready to make the trip early Monday morning.

Ever since they had arrived, Gary had been asking some of the guys from the village to come to church, but he had not been very successful. He had even asked Sid and Norm several times, but they had not shown any interest at all. But this particular Sunday morning, just before time for the services to start, the boys came sauntering up to the mission house, which was used on Sunday as a church.

Gary was on the porch when they arrived.

"Hi," Sid said. "Church started yet?"

There was a strange tone to his voice that Gary could not understand, but he replied, "You're just in time."

They came inside, grinning widely at Ross.

Gary Trumbo could not help studying them during the message. He could not make himself believe they had come because they wanted to. Yet, they seemed to be listening intently, leaning forward as though they did not want to miss a single word.

The message was simple and straightforward, a quiet presentation of the Gospel of Jesus Christ. As the meeting progressed, Gary found himself praying for Sid and Norm, asking God to work in their hearts.

He was hopeful that they would go and talk with Cliff or Danny when the service was over, but as soon as the benediction was given, they rushed outside before anyone had a chance to speak to them.

"Maybe they left so quickly because they were under conviction," Gary said to Danny. He moved thoughtfully to the window and looked out, watching Sid and Norm as they hurried down the gentle slope toward the lake. "We want to be sure to pray for them."

Ross glanced quickly at him, a miserable uncertainty reflected in his eyes, but he did not reply. The only thing he did not like about Gary Trumbo was that he was so religious and so outspoken about Christianity that there were times when Ross found it embarrassing to be with him. He knew one thing – he sure did not want to be around if Gary ever opened up on Sid and Norm. That would be the end.

Ross was pretty sure that Sid and Norm were not really interested in the Gospel but that they were just trying to make a good impression on people. They probably hoped to counteract any suspicion the townspeople might have about their activities the night of the fire. Ross had done the same thing many times himself.

Arturo seemed obsessed with the idea of finishing the film as hurriedly as possible. He insisted that Gary and Ross be out at five o'clock on Monday morning so they could start hauling equipment across the lake to the island.

"We'll be going over to that little river I showed

you the last time we were shooting on the mainland in this area," he said, pointing to a squiggly line on the map. "By the time you get things ready on the island, we'll be finished at the river and be ready to join you."

The boys had not been out on the lake more than thirty minutes or so when Del went out to the mission's aircraft, checked it over carefully, and made ready to leave.

"Is everything OK?" Danny Orlis asked.

"Everything checks out, except that she's using a little more oil than I like."

They talked about the problem briefly. Danny was always cautious and had trained Del to be the same, just as he trained all of his students. The oil use did not seem excessive, so he told Del to go ahead.

"When we get back to Rock Point we can tear into her and install new rings," suggested Del.

The instructor agreed.

While Del was waiting for the engine to warm up, he checked the controls once more and noted the gas level. The tanks were not full, but there was twice as much as he would need to get down to the town where he was to pick up the new gasoline supply.

Once the temperature gauges registered operable levels, he moved the float plane out into the lake and turned into the wind to take off. With its light load, the aircraft responded quickly. She began to increase speed, and with a surge of power came up on the step and was away. Del climbed steeply until he was well above the trees, banked, and was about to set the compass for the railhead where he would be picking up the load of gasoline. Suddenly an almost imperceptible knock interrupted the even purring of the engine.

Instantly Del was alert, straining to detect the source of the knock. He carefully brought the aircraft about and headed back toward the big lake. At that instant, a sudden vibration shook the aircraft.

The plane shook convulsively as Del, fear gripping him, feathered the prop and switched off the engine. The silence was ominous and for an instant he seemed to be suspended a thousand feet above the rough terrain. The aircraft hung there, and Del had no sensation of motion, except for the sight of the forest creeping toward the rear below him.

At first, he did not even think to pray. This could not be real. He would hear Rene call him for breakfast in a minute, or Danny would come in to waken him. And at the table he would laugh with the others about his bad dream.

But it was happening. The engine had conked out, and he was going to have to make a forced landing. Carefully he trimmed the plane, keeping the nose high to lengthen the glide. Then, gently moving the controls, he headed back to the village.

There was an eerie sense of unreality about angling to the lake with the engine off. The only sound was that of the wind rushing by on either side of the cabin, and even that was muted.

By now he was praying quietly, confidently. He knew what to do in such a situation. He had rehearsed every move until it was mechanical.

Del was surprised at his own calmness, his lack of concern. So this was what making a forced landing was like. He had often wondered when it would happen to him and how he would react. A sense of competence swept over him.

He noted his altitude and speed. The altitude was dropping and the speed increasing, but not at an alarming rate. He had only a mile to glide before he would be able to set down on the lake, and another three quarters of a mile before he reached the village. Now he knew why Danny had hammered at him so much about maintaining altitude, especially when he was flying over isolated areas.

On the ground, Gary and Ross heard the engine miss and conk out. Danny and Cliff had heard it, too. They ran down to the water's edge and stared in the direction of the small float plane. A prayer filled Danny's heart.

"If he just keeps his cool," he murmured.

Everyone else in the village heard the engine quit and knew what had happened. They were people born to the bush plane. It was a part of their lives, like the fish and beaver and outboard motors. They, too, came out of their homes and looked up silently, fearing for the slender young man who was up there alone.

The aircraft was closer now. It was almost to the south end of the lake; floating toward them so slowly they were almost unaware of any movement at all. Del was a hundred feet or so above the trees when he passed the shoreline and was over the open lake. A cheer stirred spontaneously in their throats as they realized he had cleared the most important hurdle.

"Hang in there, Del!" Danny Orlis murmured. "Keep the nose up, but don't try to stretch the glide so far you stall out. Easy now. Easy. You're flying a plane, not moving logs." Although he was scarcely aware of it, he kept muttering directions to Del until the plane was safely on the water once more.

"He made it!" Ross shouted. "He made it!"

Danny and Gary both breathed a prayer of thanksgiving.

The aircraft came to a stop half a mile from the village, and, in spite of the shortage of fuel, several boats went out to meet him. Danny took the boys and Cliff with him. They tied a line to the aircraft and towed it to the government dock.

Del was concerned about the engine.

"Forget the engine," Danny told him. "You're safe. That's all that matters. You did a good job, Del."

Once the plane was securely tied down, Danny and Del examined the power plant. Finding the problem was not difficult.'

"Take a look at this, Del," Danny told him, pointing to a huge, jagged hole in the block. "When you knock out an engine, you do a good job of it."

There was no way of making repairs. They would have to have a new engine flown in.

"And that will take some time," Danny said. "It has to come from Vancouver."

"But what about the gas for filming?" Del asked. Danny turned to Arturo for the answer.

"I think we can make it if we don't use a single gallon we don't absolutely have to."

They tried to do some filming that afternoon, but everyone was so shaken Arturo had to retake scene after scene. Finally, he called it off for the rest of the day.

Cliff Coleman came over and apologized to him. "I'm sorry about those scenes I've been blowing," he said, "but I'm so uptight I can't seem to do anything right today."

Arturo grinned briefly. "Forget it. I'm uptight myself."

# CHAPTER 8

# THREATS

Ross Kingsley left Gary in the tent and walked restlessly along the beach. He knew what he wanted to do. He had not been fishing for a couple of weeks. It would be great to get out on the lake again and pull in a couple of big ones. But there was not much of a chance of that happening. The distance he would have to go was too far to row the cumbersome, flat-bottomed boats, and there still was so little gas in Logger's Trail that they could not spare it for sport fishing. He leaned idly against the stem of one of the boats, staring out across the water. He was still there when Sid and Norm strolled up.

"It's tough the engine of that plane was knocked out," Norm said, his mouth tightening. "It means you're stuck here if the RCMP comes back."

"So what? I don't have anything to hide."

"You'd better save that for the guys who have to

believe you. You don't have to spread it on for us. We're not goin' to squeal on you," grinned Sid.

"That's right," Norm Rhinehart continued. "If you want us to, we'll even lie for you. We'll tell 'em you couldn't have been the guy who set that fire. We'll swear that you were with us all the time."

Ross wet his lips with the tip of his tongue. Did people suspect that he had been involved in the shed fire? Could he prove that he had not? True, he had been with Gary the whole time, but Gary had been asleep. It was a pretty weak alibi.

"I don't have to have an alibi," he said with more boldness than he felt.

"We know what's goin' on around here," Sid broke in. "We know everything you've done."

"But we're not goin' to tell if you're nice to us."

"Lay off, will you?" Ross muttered. "You know as well as I do that I didn't have anything to do with that shed burning."

They laughed genially.

"We didn't come over to talk about that, anyway. We wanted to see if you'd like to go fishin' with us."

"Yeah," Norm continued. "All you've got to do is furnish the gas. We've already got the boat and motor."

Ross Kingsley's cheeks flushed.

"I guess that puts an end to the fishing trip. I don't have any gas."

"Maybe not, but you know where there's plenty. All you've got to do is get it for us."

Ross did not answer them.

They were still coaxing him when Gary came out on the front porch of the mission house and called to him. Ross turned, grateful for the interruption. "I've got to go."

"You think it over!" Sid warned under his breath.

"And don't forget!" Norm repeated. "If you want us to keep still about you, know what, you'd better be a little more helpful to us. Get it?"

In spite of the fact that no one was sure when the new engine would arrive, Danny and Del set to work dismantling the old one and getting ready to remove it from the aircraft. Arturo continued to film, trying hard not to reveal his uneasiness about the possibility of not finishing before the deadline.

Cliff Coleman was still pale from his illness, but he insisted that they continue to shoot his scenes as scheduled. He was so unsure of himself that he fumbled during the first two or three takes. Then he was able to get hold of himself, and things began to fall into place. The light was right, and people who were playing the parts did better than they ever had.

"It's going great!" the director exclaimed. "Absolutely great! If we keep this up, we'll be able to have it all in the can in plenty of time."

The sudden spurt in the filming created some problems, however. With Del and Danny working on the aircraft, Gary and Ross had to be responsible for moving the camera, generators, and lights. They started work no later than six o'clock in the morning and kept at it without letup until late at night. They were so exhausted when they were done for the day that they could think only of their sleeping bags.

"Wow!" Ross exclaimed one night. "I didn't know I could get so tired!"

He and Gary had left the house and were making their way, wearily, down to their tent when Sid and Norm approached. They wanted to talk to Ross. He was somewhat surprised, since it had been almost a week since he had seen them.

He hesitated, reluctant to talk to them. "I've got things to do."

"It'll only take a minute."

Ross did not want to talk to them, but they were insistent. By this time, he knew them well enough to know that they would get their way. Gary walked on as Ross turned aside. "OK. What is it with you guys?"

For a moment or two they waited silently, as if undecided whether or not to share what they were thinking. Norm was the first to speak.

"Come on down to the lake where we can be sure that we're alone."

Ross refused. "Sorry, no can do."

"Don't give us that stuff," Sid said roughly. "We've got to talk to you."

"Not tonight." His firm resolve melted, and he resorted to blaming Gary. "Gary will be on my neck.

Every time you guys talk to me, he about gives me the third degree trying to find out everything you said."

Sid shrugged as though it was no big problem. "No sweat. Lie to him. He's so stupid he'll never know the difference."

Ross winced at the confidence the other boy expressed when he suggested lying to Gary. There was no hesitation, no sign that he had any doubt in his mind but that Ross would do it. Disturbed and irritated he started to leave. "I'll see you around."

"Oh, no you don't!" Norm Rhinehart grasped his arm and spun him around. "We've had all of that we're puttin' up with! We want to talk to you, and we want to talk now!"

Ross tried to jerk away. "What's this all about?" he demanded, his irritation rising. "I haven't done anything to you guys."

"You haven't done anything *for* us, either!" Norm said. "That's just the trouble!"

Ross did not like the tone of Norm's voice. "Wh-what do you mean?"

"We've tried bein' nice to you, but it hasn't done any good! We decided to quit *askin'* you to get gas for us. Now we're *tellin'* you!"

So that was it. Ross might have known! "How many times do I have to tell you, I can't get any gas for you. I haven't got any! You should know that by this time."

"I didn't say you had any gas." Norm's voice was

ominously hushed. "But you know where there is some! And you know how to get it!"

Ross looked helplessly from one to the other. "I don't dare run the risk," he pleaded. "Like I told you, they'd throw the book at me if I got caught."

"Then you'd better not get caught! Did you ever think of that?"

Ross started to argue, but Norm broke in, irritably. "You'd better pay attention to what Sid says." His fingers contracted, squeezing down on Ross's arm until it was all he could do to keep from crying out. "If you don't get some gas, we'll give you a workin' over you won't forget very soon. When we get done your own mother wouldn't even know you. Understand?"

He stared from one to the other, bewildered momentarily by the threat. "You don't mean that," he murmured. "You've got to be kidding."

"Just try us!" Sid's voice was ominously quiet.

"We're not going to stand for any more excuses. You get that gas for us or–or you'll wish you had. That's a promise!"

Sweat beaded Ross's forehead. "I–I'd like to help you but I–I don't see how I can. I–."

"I'll tell you what we're goin' to do," Norm said. "We'll give you twenty-four hours to get us ten gallons of gas." He said no more, but there was no doubt about what would happen if Ross failed.

The younger boy squirmed miserably. "I'd do it

if I could," he said lamely. "Honest I would. But I've got this Gary character watching every move I make. And you know what–what a religious fanatic he is. He'd blow the whistle on all of us and get a kick out of doing it. He–."

"That's your problem!" Sid cut in. "Don't bother us with that stuff."

Ross knew, then, that he had no choice. He would have to get the gas for them, somehow. He had hoped to talk his way out of it, but it was useless. He knew what would happen to him if he did not come up with what they wanted.

"I–I might be able to get you five," he stammered, "but they'd be sure to miss ten gallons. And if they did, right away they'd go after whoever took it! They're gettin' so low now that they almost dole it out by the quart."

Sid and Norm finally decided to let him off if he'd get five gallons for them.

"OK. OK." Norm made it sound as though he was the most generous person in the village. "But you've only got one chance to get it for us. You hand over five gallons of gas to us by tomorrow night – or else!"

Ross remained motionless, staring into the distance for a time after they left him. He did not want to steal the gas. He had decided long ago that he would never get involved in anything like that again. He knew, now, where it would get him. But he did not know what to do about Sid and Norm, either. The more he thought about them and their threats, the more convinced he became that he had to do what they wanted him to. Either one of them was a lot bigger than he was, and he had to face *both* of them.

A lot of guys just pretended to be tough. He had met plenty of that kind back home in Rock Point. Stand up to them once or twice and they would back off. But not these two! They meant what they said. Ross trembled inside, just thinking about them.

Ross felt that he really did not have a choice. He had to follow their wishes. But, he promised himself, he was doing it only this one time. And another thing – he was not going fishing with them anymore or having anything else to do with them. The less he was around them, the better.

He would have to take the gas without asking. He knew that. But he was going to figure out some way of paying the mission for what he took. He did not have any money right then, but he was going to find some way to pay for it.

He still had not moved when Sid came back to him, sidling up as though he was Ross's best friend. "I wanted to tell you that all of this is Norm's idea," he whispered. "It's not mine."

Ross did not answer him.

"And I know what you're up against as far as Gary Trumbo is concerned. I've talked with him a few times. He's far out on this religion kick."

"You can say that again," Ross replied.

Sid lowered his voice even more than before. "I know what a rough time you'll have getting away from him. If you go alone, he'll give you all sorts of guff, but he won't think anything about it if the two of us go fishing."

Ross had to agree to that. "But what's that got to do with getting the gas for you and Norm?" he asked.

"Don't you see? We'll pretend to go fishing, and while we're gone, we can clip over and get the gas you promised Norm. How about that?"

# CHAPTER 9

# A DECEITFUL DEED

At first Ross was excited about the opportunity to get away from Gary. He had been deeply concerned about how he could manage to lose his pal long enough to go out to the island to get the gas. Going with Sid would be a lot easier than trying to avoid Gary on his own.

There was only one thing wrong with Sid's scheme. In order to bring it off, he would have to let Sid know where the gas was hidden. And if that happened, none of the film crew's meager supply would be safe. Maybe Sid was his friend as he said. But Ross knew him and Norm well enough to suspect they would go back to the island on their own and make off with every gallon of gas if they learned where it was hidden. Then there would not be any way the mission could get the film finished! They had to have fuel to run the generator and to transport equipment.

He shook his head. "Nope. I think I'd better go alone."

The other boy bristled. "What kind of a guy are you?" he demanded. "I try to help you, and you won't even let me."

"I–I know," he stammered defensively, "but I–I have an idea how to do it, now. I don't think I'll need any help from anyone."

That really was not the truth. He did not have a clue as to how he could get away from Gary long enough to get out to the island and back. The only thing he knew for sure was that he could not let Sid and Norm find out where the gas supply was hidden. He had a feeling that was what Sid really wanted. They would not go to all that trouble for only five gallons. They wanted to find out where the rest of it was stored so they could take what was left.

Sid managed to mask his frustration and anger.

"I should let Norm work you over. That's what I really should do, but I hate to see that happen. I'd like to help you if I can. I'll tell you what I'll do. If you'll tell me where the gas is stored, I'll go out and get the five gallons myself. That way you won't have to get involved. Norm will never need to know any-thing about it."

"I made a deal," Ross said. "I'll stick to it."

"That's just the point. We're willing to let you off the hook if you tell me where the gas is. That's all I ask."

"No way. I'm not letting you or anybody else know where the gas is stashed, so forget it."

Sid continued to press, but finally he became convinced that it was useless. He scowled. "OK, I'll let it go until tomorrow night. But I'm warnin' you! If you don't have that gas before your time is up, you're goin' to tell us where it's hidden or else!"

Ross shuddered as the other boy stormed away. He did not want to go back to the tent and face Gary, but he could not stay out any longer. Norm might be the one who came back the next time. He had to go someplace where they would not bother him. He turned miserably and stumbled back to the tent.

That night sleep was elusive. He thought about Sid and Norm constantly, and every time he closed his eyes he could see their faces. Once or twice, he felt that he had to confide in Gary, but he decided he could not do that. If he did, he would be in a real fix. Gary would never go along with stealing that gas, and if he did not get it for Norm, he did not dare to think about what would happen.

The next day was as busy as the others. Ross was so preoccupied, he kept making mistakes. He saw that Arturo was irritated, although he was trying to be patient. But how could he help making mistakes? He had to have that gas for Norm and Sid by evening, and he still did not know how he was going to get it.

The easiest thing, he had decided, would be to steal it when they were over on the island. But there seemed no way to manage it. Everybody was there, for one thing. He could not fill a five-gallon can without getting caught. And if he could manage that much, he would not be able to sneak it into the boat to take it back to the village. He had to have some other way of doing the job.

On the way back to Logger's Trail, the shooting over for the day, Ross decided on a course of action. He did not like the idea of lying to Gary, but he did not like the idea of being beat up, either.

"I want to talk to you as soon as we get back," he told his pal. He knew the right tone to put in his voice.

As soon as they tied the boat to the dock and had the gear unloaded the two boys went off together.

"Now, what did you want to talk to me about?" Gary asked him.

"I–I've been doing a lot of thinking about–about what you've told me about confessing my sin and putting my trust in Jesus Christ. Would you mind going over it again?"

Gary got out his Testament and read a number of verses to Ross – verses that explained why he had to acknowledge that he was a sinner and put his trust in Christ for salvation.

Ross questioned him at length and finally said that he had to do some serious thinking. "I think I–I'd like to be alone for a while to sort of reason some of these things out, in my own way."

Gary nodded understandingly.

Then Ross asked the one question he had been leading up to. "Do you think it would be alright for me to take the boat out for a while? I'd just like to go someplace where I won't be bothered." He asked the question fearfully. If Gary said no, he was sunk.

Gary hesitated. The boys were not allowed to go out in the boat alone without first asking permission. "Let me just check it out with Danny," he said.

He ran up to the mission house and was soon back again. "Danny says it's OK, as long as you don't stay out on the lake after dark. There are some hidden rocks, and it would be too dangerous."

Ross breathed a sigh of relief and left as quickly as he could, taking his jacket and heading down to the boat. A great uneasiness seized him as he headed out into the open lake. He did not like this business. He did not like anything about it. But he was locked into it now; he could not get out of it.

He wanted to get over to the island, and pick up the gas, and return as quickly as possible, but he would have to be careful. He did not dare to open the throttle and head straight for the island. If he did that, he would have a lot of questions to answer when he got back.

He kept the throttle at half speed, heading in the direction opposite from the island. He had two things to consider. Gary was smart, for one thing. He would be sure to notice if the motor sounded as if the boat were heading straight toward the island where they had been filming, and he would wonder about it.

Also, there was Sid and Norm. Those characters just might not be satisfied with five gallons of gas. They might try to follow him. And the worst of it was that in the night stillness they would be able to hear his motor from quite a distance. They would not have to follow close behind him; they could let the sound guide them. And in the growing gloom, he would have a hard time even knowing if they were trailing him.

Every now and then he shut off his motor and listened intently. There was no sound of any other outboards on the broad lake, however. All he could hear was the breathless hush of the evening, marred only by the haunting melody of a distant loon calling to his mate.

When Ross was sure he was far enough away to avoid being heard or seen, he shoved the throttle wide open and headed directly for the island.

When he reached the island, he filled a five-gallon can with gas from one of the barrels. He was about to leave when he remembered that he had gone so far that he had used quite a lot of gas himself. The film director would be sure to notice if the tank was almost empty.

He went back and got enough gas to fill the tank enough that no one would be suspicious. He paused for a moment, going over his actions in his mind.

He could not think of anything he had left undone that would give him away. Satisfied, he got in the boat and headed for the mainland.

As he neared the dock, a sudden fear came over him. What if Gary came down to meet him before he got the gas to Sid and Norm?

But that did not happen. He was tying up the mission boat when Norm and his companion appeared on the dock. "Well, I see you went for your boat ride." There was a derisive, mocking tone in his voice.

Ross found it difficult to answer him. "Yeah, and I–I've got something for you." Ross hoped that they would not guess where he had gone to get the gas. He reassured himself with the thought that there were several islands on the large lake, as well as many bays and inlets. The gasoline drums could be hidden in any number of places.

"Well now, that makes good sense. That makes real good sense." Norm grinned. "Now we know where to go whenever we need gas."

Ross Kingsley winced. They had promised to let him off the hook if he got gas for them once, but they were not going to. He knew they would keep coming to him, threatening if he refused to get more gas for them.

"That's not what you promised!" he exclaimed. Norm's laugh rang out on the still night air.

"We didn't make any promises, did we, Sid?"

"Not that I know of."

"But don't let it shake you up," Norm added. "We're going to treat you right. Unless we get in another jam and absolutely *have* to have more gas, we won't bother you."

Ross checked the mission boat to be sure it was securely tied and stumbled wearily in the direction of the tent. He might have known this would happen. Sid and Norm were not going to let him off the hook. He would have to face them again in two or three days. But that would not be the end of it, either. They would keep coming back to him until he got caught, or the gas was gone, or the film crew finished work and he was able to leave the village. It would be even harder for him to turn them down now that he had given in to them once. They knew he had a breaking point and would keep pressing him until he did what they wanted. He was in a mess that would never end!

Gary had crawled into his bedroll but was still awake when Ross opened the flap and crawled into the tent. He rolled over on his side and sat up.

"I'm glad you're back. I was beginning to worry about you."

"I–I guess I stayed a little longer than I should have."

Gary was understanding.

"No problem. I was just afraid you might be having some trouble. If you hadn't come back in another fifteen or twenty minutes, I'd have gotten Danny or Del to go out on the lake with me to look for you."

A vague uneasiness swept over Ross. He had not even considered that possibility. And to think! He would probably have to run that risk again.

"Did you get things sorted out in your mind?" Gary asked.

At first Ross did not understand what he meant.

"You know. You said you wanted to think about letting Jesus Christ have control of your life."

"Oh – that. No. I–I didn't decide anything."

"Would you like to have me pray with you?" Gary asked him.

Ross's temper flared. "When I want you to pray for me, I'll tell you!"

He pulled off his shoes and socks, keeping his back to Gary. He was glad it was dark in the tent. He would not have to explain why his hands were trembling. He had never felt so helpless or so miserable and unclean in his entire life.

# CHAPTER 10

# CAUGHT IN THE ACT

Ross Kingsley knew that Sid and Norm would be coming after him again and tried to keep out of their way. That, however, was impossible. They knew when he left the village with the film crew and could see him when he came back. They were at the dock waiting for him two days later and called him aside.

"Are you guys out of your mind?" he asked softly. "You're going to get all three of us in plenty of trouble coming around in front of Danny and Cliff and Del."

"You sound as though you're ashamed of us," Sid said.

"It hurts to have you turn against us that way." Norm paused. "Especially when there was something wrong with that gas you got for us."

"What do you mean?"

"There was something wrong with it. It didn't last at all," Sid added.

"That's right." The bigger of the two came up close to Ross. "We've got to have some more."

"But you told me you wouldn't ask me to–to steal any more gas for you," he repeated defensively. "You gave me your word."

"We didn't ask him to steal any gas, did we, Norm?"

"Of course not. We wouldn't ask him to do a terrible thing like that. He just volunteered to get some gas for us because we were kind enough to take him fishing with us. Remember?"

Ross's eyes flashed. "Don't try to lie your way out of it!"

Norm grasped him by the arm. "Take it easy!" he hissed. "Half the people in the village will hear you if you keep this up!"

"You're going to get some more gas for us, or you'll wish you had! We're warning you!"

"Go ahead and warn me!" he retorted hotly. "I don't care what you say! I'm not goin' out where those bears are and get any gas for you!"

The instant he spoke he recoiled and his face paled. *What had he done?*

"Now I know where that gas is hidden!" Sid exclaimed, triumphantly. "It's out on the island where you were doing some filming and had all that stuff messed up by the grizzlies!" He turned to Norm. "That's where it is! We don't need him anymore!"

Ross managed a weak little laugh. "Who said anything about the gas being on that island?"

"You did."

"I didn't mean that," he lied. "I–."

Norm turned his back on him. "Come on, Sid. We can get our own gas."

Dismay swept over Ross as the other two boys dashed over to their boat and shoved it into the water. Now everything was all messed up. Sid and Norm knew where the gas supply was hidden. They would steal all of it, and that would ruin the filming!

He still had not moved when Sid, who was at the controls, brought the cumbersome, flat-bottomed boat about and headed across the lake. Ross shuddered. He had ruined everything!

Mechanically Ross turned back to the mission boat. He should have known that he would not be able to stop them alone. But there was no time for regret. All he knew was that his supposed friends were going to steal their gas unless he did something.

He dashed off the dock, jumped lightly to the beach, and ran over to the mission boat. He dug his feet into the wet sand and threw all his strength against the boat, trying to move it back into the water. He shoved until the veins stood out on his temples and the backs of his hands and his knees were trembling. The boat moved protestingly on the log rollers towards the water, a few grudging inches at a time.

"Dear God, help me to get this boat into the water and–." It surprised him that he would even try to pray. How could he expect God to hear his prayers?

This mess was all his own doing. He was the one who had ruined everything. He could not expect God to help him get things straightened out again.

"Hey!" Gary sang out at that moment. He was running across the beach toward Ross. "Where're you goin?"

Ross had not thought he would be glad to see his pal in such circumstances, but he was. "Come on! Give me a hand! We've got to get out to the island, quick!"

By this time Gary was at his side. "What gives?"

"It's Sid and Norm! They're headed for the island where we've got the gas hidden. They're going to steal it unless we stop 'em!"

Gary did not understand. "They don't even know it's there!"

"They do now. I was stupid enough to let it slip." Hurriedly he related what had happened a few minutes before, leaving out the references to his own involvement. He took the blame for letting the location of the fuel slip out, but that was all. He said nothing about the gas he had taken or the fact that they tried to pressure him into stealing more from the film crew's meager supply. "I don't know what was the matter with me," he lied boldly. "They were begging me to tell them where the gas was. I wasn't going to do it, but they kept bugging me until I got mad and it slipped out."

"What happened then?" Gary asked.

"About what you'd imagine. As soon as they heard me mention the island where we tangled with the bears, they knew where it was and took off. We've got to get out there, or they'll take the gas that's left and we'll be in an awful jam."

"How long ago did they leave?" Gary wanted to know. Looking up, however, he had the answer to his own question. Half a mile out on the lake he could see the other two boys heading straight for the island in their boat. "We'd better go back and get Danny and Cliff!" he exclaimed.

Ross Kingsley did not want to take the time to go and get Danny Orlis or anyone else. He did not want to have to talk to them, either. Not right then. They just might have some embarrassing questions that he would have trouble answering.

"We can't wait to do that," he protested. "Sid and Norm've got too big a lead on us as it is. We've got to hurry, or we won't get over there in time to stop them."

In spite of the lead the local boys had on them, Gary refused to take the boat without seeing Danny.

When Ross saw that he was determined to do so, he started to run up the hill in the direction of the mission house.

"Come on, then! Let's get with it!"

Gary followed him a dozen steps or so before he stopped, groaning miserably.

"It won't do any good to go back to the house.

They all hiked over to the abandoned mine to see if it would be a good place to shoot a few fill-in scenes they just worked into the script."

Ross came to a stop. "We can't wait any longer, or it won't do any good to go over there!"

"We know who they are," Gary told him. "Danny or Cliff can call the RCMP."

Inwardly Ross was trembling. If that happened, Sid and Norm would squeal on him, and he would be in trouble with them. There *had* to be some other way.

"What good would that do? They'd deny they'd taken the gas, and the chances are they'd have it hidden so well nobody could find it. So it would just be our word against theirs!"

Reluctantly Gary admitted that what Ross said was true. He did not like the idea of taking the mission boat without asking. Ordinarily he would not, even though Cliff and Danny had always allowed them to use it any time they wanted to. If they were going to catch Sid and Norm before they got away with the gas, they would have to get started right away. They could not wait until Danny came back to the village.

"OK, let's get that boat in the water and get going."

Together they worked the heavy mission boat into the lake and scrambled into it. Ross was staring into the distance. Already Sid and Norm were out of sight.

"I hope we can get there in time," he murmured.

Ross started the big engine and twisted the throttle in the handle until the outboard was screaming at top voice. The prop was churning the water wildly in an effort to shove the massive boat fast enough to suit its occupants. The heavy scow plowed a deep furrow in the still water, leaving a widening wake behind.

Gary, who had taken his place in the stem, twisted about to stare at the distant horizon. He tried to make himself believe he could see the other boat, but he could not. Only emptiness lay ahead.

Ross turned the handle as hard as possible in an effort to coax a little more speed from the engine, but the craft only crept along. Surely it was not running wide open he told himself. The boat went faster than that with a full load. There *had* to be some way of getting more speed out of it. Gary, too, felt that they were not getting all the speed they ought.

"They're going to be over there and have the gas and be gone again before we get halfway across the lake," he complained. "That's what gets me so uptight."

Ross nodded, but he did not speak aloud. He was not anxious to face Sid and Norm, even with Gary along, but they had to. They had to stop them if they could!

They were a mile or so from the island when Gary stood up and peered intently at the white beach. A moment before he thought he had seen something move on shore, a blurred figure that could have been one of the guys. As they drew closer, however, he recognized the dark shape as only a deadhead washed up by the waves. Behind it was a bush that showed ominously black against the lighter green of the poplar and birch around it.

"See any sign of those guys?" Ross wanted to know.

"Nope. They aren't on this side. Maybe they haven't gotten here yet."

Ross could not believe that to be true. Sid and Norm had had plenty of time to make it over to the island.

"Maybe they changed their minds," Gary suggested. "Or they might not have really meant to steal the gas. Do you suppose they were just putting you on?"

Ross wanted to believe that, but he knew Sid and Norm too well. They were not putting him on.

The boys beached the mission boat quickly and hurried over to where the gasoline drums were cached. Ross was in the lead, crashing through the underbrush.

"It's still here!" he sang out triumphantly to Gary, who was still far behind.

At that instant Sid and Norm stepped out of the brush, grinning broadly.

"Well, now, look who's here. It was so nice of you to come all this way to help us get the barrels down to the beach so we can load 'em."

"It was real thoughtful of you," Norm said. "You make us sorry for all the bad things we said about you on the way over here. Come on, now, and give us a hand."

Gary, who had stopped running at the sound

of the voices, came out from the bushes and stood beside Ross.

"Hi."

They stared at him. "What're you doing here?" Norm demanded.

"We heard that a couple of guys were planning to steal our gas, so we came to see about it." Gary spoke calmly, as if confronting would-be thieves was something he and Ross did every day. But there was also steel in his voice, a hard tone of warning.

That seemed to startle Sid and Norm.

"Who's stealin'?" Sid demanded angrily. "We just came out to get the gas Ross sold us." He turned threateningly to Ross Kingsley. "Ain't that right?"

"Sure it is," Norm protested when he saw that Ross would say nothing. "He sold us five gallons of gas a couple of nights ago, and when we talked to him today, he said we'd have to come after it ourselves if we wanted anymore."

"That's the truth!" Sid muttered. "We'll swear to it."

"You don't have to work so hard trying to get me to believe it. The ones you have to convince are the RCMP."

At the mention of the Mounties Sid and Norm looked warily at each other.

"You–you wouldn't turn us in, would you?" Norm asked plaintively.

"You'd better believe it. As soon as we get back

to the village, we're telling Danny and Cliff about this. And they'll call the RCMP. That's a promise."

Sid's fists clenched.

"You'd better think a long time about squealing on us. If you say anything to anyone, you'll get the worst beating you ever had."

"That's exactly right," Norm blustered. "So the best thing you can do is to forget all of this ever happened."

Gary did not move. "Nothing doing."

Sid pushed close to him. "You don't want that pretty face of yours messed up, do you?"

Gary Trumbo stood his ground. "I'm not much on starting fights," he said quietly, "but you'll make a bad mistake if you decide we won't defend ourselves."

Norm swung at him, a long, looping right to the face. Gary jerked his head to one side, so the fist only struck a glancing blow on his cheek. With a sudden, cat-like movement Gary grasped his assailant's wrist, twisting his arm and bringing it up behind his back.

"Ouch!" Norm cried.

Sid sprang forward to help his pal, but Ross jumped in front of him. "You leave them alone!"

Sid stopped uncertainly. In that instant of hesitation, Gary and Ross both knew that they had won.

"We didn't mean nothing," Norm Rhinehart sulked. "You don't need to get so uptight about it. We weren't goin' to steal the gas. We were only goin' to hide one of the barrels so you'd think we'd taken it, that's all. We wouldn't be so dumb as to steal gas – especially when the Mounties are comin' back out here. We don't want to have no trouble with them."

Gary did not relax his grip on Norm's arm. "Let's go down to your boat, shall we?"

He marched Norm ahead of him and Sid followed along, two or three steps behind. Ross was not far away.

"We'll get you, Ross," Sid muttered under his breath. "This is all your fault, and we'll get you for it. Just remember that."

# CHAPTER 11

# STRANDED!

At the boat Sid and Norm protested their innocence once more and tried to make Gary agree not to tell anyone about their visit to the island. Gary was not even listening to them, however, and they both knew it.

"I don't know why you have to be so stupid," Sid murmured as he and Norm pushed their boat back into the water and got in.

Ross and Gary stood watching on the beach until the other craft disappeared from view. "Now, where do you think they're going?" Ross asked when he saw that Sid and Norm had not started back across the lake in the direction of the village.

Gary shrugged.

"Think they'll come back here and try again?" Gary Trumbo had been thinking about that. It did not seem likely. He had the impression that they would be afraid to, but it was too important a matter just to assume that they would not be back.

"I doubt that they'll dare come over here again," he said, "but I don't think we should leave for a while yet. They just might hang around nearby to see if we take off right away."

They talked it over and decided that Gary would stay to guard the gas while Ross took the boat and went back to get Danny or Del.

"What about those grizzlies?" Ross asked. "What're you going to do if they come back?"

Gary pulled in his breath sharply. He had not thought about them. He tried to block them out of his mind as he and Ross made their way back to the beach where they had left their boat.

"Just don't stay any longer than you have to, Ross," he cautioned.

Ross was looking up and down the beach. It was empty!

"Where's our boat?"

"Sid and Norm must've come back and taken it!"

The boys eyed each other with growing helplessness. They were stranded on the island, alone with the bears!

* * *

Danny, Arturo, and Cliff hiked over to the abandoned mine, decided it would be suitable for shooting the scenes the director needed, and returned to the mission house shortly after six o'clock in the evening. Rene had the evening meal ready.

"I guess we're ready to eat," she said. "Why don't you have the boys come in and get washed, Danny?"

He looked at her blankly. "Where are they?"

"Weren't they with you?"

"We haven't seen them all afternoon." He turned to Del and asked him to go out and find Gary and Ross.

The others waited twenty minutes, but when Del still had not returned they sat down to eat. They were just finishing when he came in and announced that he had been unable to locate the boys.

"Jonas told me he saw them take the mission boat and head across the lake."

"That doesn't sound like Gary," Danny remarked.

"They sure aren't in the village."

Danny's forehead crinkled, revealing his concern.

* * *

Out on the island Ross looked at Gary quickly and then looked away. He did not want to reveal the fear that was churning within him. Darkness was descending on the lake, and with the coming of darkness, they would not be able to see the grizzlies.

"Wh-what'll we do, Gary?" he asked uncertainly.

"The only thing we can do is wait until Danny or somebody realizes we're gone and comes out looking for us."

That did not sound good to Ross. "Do–do you think they'll come tonight?"

Gary was not sure about that. Darkness was already upon them, and the big lake was full of reefs and great boulders lurking a few inches below the surface. He doubted that they would risk going out until daylight.

"And if we have to stay here until tomorrow," Ross continued, "what are we going to do about those grizzlies?"

"You heard what Cliff said about them. They keep moving around. We don't even know that there are any bears out here now."

That was little encouragement.

"Maybe we don't," Ross said. "And maybe they're having a convention out here, too. There may be twice as many of them here as there were when they wrecked the inside of that cabin and ruined all our food."

Gary laughed uneasily. When he thought about those bears, he did not feel much better than his companion did. "You sure are a bundle of light."

They went over to the clearing not far from the place where the gas barrels were hidden and hurriedly began to gather wood. There was a lot of dead wood on the ground, but Gary insisted on pulling dead branches from the trees.

"They're drier and will burn better," he explained.

"What're we getting all this wood for?" Ross asked.

"Don't you know? Fire will keep bears away."

Ross stared suspiciously at him. "You're puttin' me on."

"That's the truth."

Ross Kingsley's fingers were trembling as he took some matches from his pocket and struck one. Moments later the flames were crackling merrily.

"A fire does make a guy feel better, doesn't it?" he remarked aloud.

They sat down, cross-legged, in front of the fire, drawing warmth and confidence from the flames. For several minutes neither boy spoke.

"I'm glad we were able to stop Sid and Norm before they stole the gas," Gary said at last. "I'd sure hate to see them get into a jam for stealing."

Ross picked up a stick and began to poke at the fire nervously. For an instant remorse swept over him. He was the one who was in a jam, when it came to stealing gas. He had slipped over to the island and had taken five gallons to give to Sid and Norm.

True, they had threatened him to make him get the gas for them, but it was his word against theirs when it came to that. Did Gary know or suspect anything? If so, Ross knew that he would have a lot of explaining to do as soon as they got back to Logger's Trail.

"I keep thinking about the service those guys went to last Sunday," Gary continued. "If they'd turned their hearts over to Christ when Cliff was speaking, they wouldn't have done what they did this evening. Everything would be so much better for them and for us."

Ross shuddered. It was not the fact that Sid and Norm had not made decisions for Jesus Christ that disturbed him. He was thinking about his own relationship with Christ. He was not a Christian himself. That was the reason he was in this jam.

* * *

Danny said little to the others about the boys' disappearance, but concern was beginning to weigh on him. In all the time Gary had been staying with him and Kay, he had not known him to go off without telling one of them where he was going.

Cliff was more concerned about the boys' knowledge of the bush. "Does either of them know how to take care of himself in this kind of country?"

"I doubt that Ross has been around very much, but Gary should be able to do about as well as any guy his age who wasn't born up here."

"Then I don't think there's any reason to worry. They'll find their way back without any trouble."

Danny was not reassured. "It isn't like Gary to go off this way without telling anyone where he was going and when he planned to be back. I'm afraid there's something wrong."

"Of course, if the fish started hitting the boys might have forgotten all about time," Cliff reminded him. "I've planned on going out for an hour or so and wound up spending half a day."

"So have I, but I still can't buy that as the reason for the boys being gone tonight. I don't think Gary would have gone fishing without running up to the house and telling Rene or scribbling a note for us."

The men talked it over and decided to wait awhile before going out to look for the boys. While they were waiting, they went over to the Trading Post and made arrangements to borrow the storekeeper's boat. Del went to find Sid and Norm, hoping to get some information about Gary and Ross from them.

* * *

Shortly after the sun went down, a harsh wind stormed out of the north. It snarled through the treetops and sent long, deep-troughed breakers crashing into the rocks and along the beach that lined much of the island. Ross and Gary could not see the lake from where they were sitting, but they did not have to see the wild water to know what was happening. They could hear the rhythmic thunder of waves crashing against the rocks and could see the trees bending before the brutal onslaught of the wind.

The fire licked out crazily in the wind. The boys hastily cleared away all of the brush and twigs around the fire. When they had cleared a large area of dirt around the fire, they were satisfied that it would not have a chance to go out of control.

"I hope Sid and Norm got back before this hit," Gary said uneasily. "It's bad out there."

Something in his tone drove a spear of remorse into Ross Kingsley's consciousness. Grimly, he pushed it aside. They were faced with more important problems than whether Sid and Norm got caught out on the lake in the storm. They had to worry about the approaching darkness and the grizzlies.

"If this keeps up," he said nervously, "it's sure that we'll be stuck here all night."

Gary had been thinking the same thing but had not voiced his fear. There was no reason to become any more upset than they were already.

But Ross was not willing to push aside his uneasiness. "What're we going to do?" he. asked.

Gary shrugged. "Danny and Cliff will find us, sooner or later."

"And just exactly how are they going to do that?" Ross demanded. "This wind could blow for a week. You know that, don't you?"

Gary was about to reply when a strong, pungent odor pinched at his nostrils – an odor he had only smelled once or twice in his entire life. He stood uncertainly and took a step or two forward, staring intently into the darkening brush.

"What's wrong?" Ross asked, curiously. Then he caught the odor, too, and recognized it from the other occasion when they spent the night on the island. "Bears!"

Gary nodded. "They're out there, all right, but the fire will keep them away!"

"You hope."

Gary went back to the fire and sat down. He had to admit that he was disturbed by the knowledge that the grizzlies were out there, just beyond the trees and brush. Anyone who knew anything at all about the ill-tempered animals warned against being careless around them. Still, he was not going to panic.

"We prayed that God would take care of us," he said. "Now we've got to trust Him."

The other boy's temper flared suddenly. "Yeah, that's easy for you to say," he blurted. "You *know* Christ is going to take care of you."

Only then did he realize how he had given himself away. He had drawn back the curtain to allow Gary to see that he was really troubled by his lack of a personal relationship with Christ.

"You don't have to leave it that way," Gary said quietly. "You can get it settled right now – tonight."

"It's alright for you to talk that way, but you don't know what I've done." Remorse broke his voice.

"When it gets right down to it, Ross, that doesn't make any difference to God," Gary told him. If he was shocked by his pal's statement, he did not show it. "He specializes in guys who are sinners. And that's all of us."

"I don't get that," he countered. "What do you mean by it?"

"God doesn't say we have to be *good* enough to be saved. If that were the case, none of us would make it. We've got to admit that we're sinners and can't do anything about getting our lives straightened out on our own before God can help us. He says He will save us if we confess our sin and put our trust in Him."

Ross still had difficulty believing that God actually meant to include guys like him. "But I–." He stopped, uneasily, and began again. "But I've done a lot of things you don't even know about." He went on to tell his pal how he had stolen gas for Sid and Norm. "I didn't want to do it. I tried everything I could think of to get out of doing it, but they put the heat on me so much that I–." He gestured helplessly.

Gary Trumbo was surprised to learn that his friend had stolen again, but Ross was wrong about God not forgiving him.

"That's one thing you don't have to worry about," he explained. "God has forgiven a lot of things that are worse than anything you've done. All He cares about is that you're truly sorry for what you've done and that you really mean business about letting Him straighten out your life. Then you can live for Him."

Ross turned that over in his mind, thoughtfully. He guessed he had not really understood how it was. He had always thought he had to get his life cleaned up on his own and then come to God. But that was not how Gary was explaining it.

He reached out and stirred the fire. Now that

he thought about it, there was something else that troubled him. "What do you mean, 'mean business'? How do you do that?" he asked.

Gary had to think about that for a time. He knew what he had to say; the difficulty was in knowing just how to say it.

"A guy's got to make things right if he can."

Ross was not sure he liked the sound of that. "What do you mean?"

"Let's talk about that gas you stole. If you're going to mean business with God, you've got to ask Him to forgive you. Then you've got to go to Danny and Arturo and confess what you did and work out some way of paying them for it."

"But I can't do that!" the other boy exclaimed. "You know the RCMP are supposed to be coming back. If I tell Danny what I've done, he'll turn me over to the Mounties."

Gary did not answer him directly. He did not think Danny would have Ross arrested, but that was not the problem right then. "The question you've got to ask yourself is this: Do I want to be forgiven? If you do, you've got to confess things like stealing that gas. There isn't any other way. God will forgive your sins, but He will also give you a desire to have forgiveness from the people you have wronged."

Ross was close to tears as he knelt near the fire.

Gary knelt beside him.

# CHAPTER 12

# ROSS SETS THINGS STRAIGHT

Once Ross Kingsley's tongue was loosed, the words tumbled out frantically as he opened his heart and asked God's forgiveness. Neither he nor Gary knew how long they remained on their knees. Time seemed irrelevant as they talked to God.

They were just getting to their feet when they heard a chilling, deep-throated growl from the brush nearby. They looked up quickly.

"Did you hear that?" Ross demanded.

Gary nodded wordlessly. How could he keep from hearing it? It rumbled through to the very depths of his being.

"I thought you said the fire would keep those bears away!"

For the first time since they began to talk about Ross's personal relationship with Jesus Christ, they noticed the fire. The wood was charred and all but enveloped in ashes. Starved of fuel, the fire had almost died. A feeble glow came from the dying embers.

"It's almost out," Gary said.

The boys set to work immediately, building the fire up once more. Ross stirred the coals until the flames brightened, and Gary piled dry wood on them. It was not long until the fire was crackling upward again, doing battle with the darkness that surrounded them.

Ross listened for bears, but he could hear nothing except the crackle of the flames and the sound of the waves breaking over the rocks. The fire was actually keeping the bears away! He relaxed slightly, managing a weak grin.

"Know something?" he exclaimed. "This is the best fire I've ever been around in my life!"

Gary had to agree. He also found comfort in the bright flames. Then he noticed something that disturbed him. "Take a look at our wood supply. It's not going to last all night, that's for sure."

"We can go out and get some more, can't we?" Ross asked.

"I've just been thinking about that." The muscles about Gary's mouth tightened. "I don't know whether we dare risk it or not. We don't have a flashlight, and with those bears so close it won't be safe to go out very far to get any more firewood. We'll have to wait until daylight when we can watch for those grizzlies."

"What're we going to do?" Ross asked apprehensively.

Gary got to his feet, quietly praying for guidance, and walked to the edge of the faint circle of light. There he stopped as if weighing his chances of going after more wood and getting back safely.

"There is something somebody told me about grizzlies once. He told me there is a way to keep them away."

"Great! What is it?"

"I don't even know if it works or not."

"We can find that out soon enough!" Ross cried. "What is it?"

"Get a couple of those sticks of firewood and come over here."

"Hold the phone! If you think I'm about to club one of those bears on the nose, you're out of your mind."

"Nobody's talking about clubbing any bears on the nose."

* * *

Del Davis had a little difficulty finding Sid and Norm. He went to the Trading Post first, and when old Jonas said he had not seen them, he looked for the boys at their homes. But their parents had not seen them for several hours, either.

Del saw that the wind was beginning to come up, and it concerned him. He knew enough about big bodies of water to know how rough it could get in a storm. If Gary and Ross were out on the lake, they could be in plenty of trouble. He was about to give up looking for Sid and Norm when he saw their boat come in to the dock. He went down to talk to them. At first, they claimed they had not seen Gary and Ross all day.

"You were the only ones out on the lake except Gary and Ross. They headed out across the open lake not long after you did."

"How do you know?" Norm broke in.

"The mission boat's gone, for one thing. And for another, Jonas saw you and Gary and Ross."

"Oh–." Sid's expression changed as if he just remembered. "Now that I think of it, we did see them. They were heading for the island."

"But I don't think they're coming home tonight," Norm blurted. "I got the idea they were staying all night."

Del was not satisfied with the explanation the other boy gave, but he felt it would be useless to ask more questions. He went back to Danny and Cliff with the information he had just learned. The three were still talking when the wind swooped in, screeching through the trees and lashing furiously at the big body of water. Cliff squinted out across the white-splashed water.

"There goes our chance of getting out to the island and trying to find them tonight," he murmured.

Danny glanced up at the sky. "I think you're right,"

he said at last. "We shouldn't risk our own necks and take a chance on losing the boat on a reef in the dark."

They were not concerned about the fact that the boys would have to spend the night outdoors. That would not hurt either of them. But the grizzlies were another matter. Neither Danny nor Cliff mentioned the bears, but they could think of little else. Those big animals were so ill-tempered, so unpredictable, no one could be sure what they would or would not do.

Two or three times before going to bed that night Danny Orlis went to the window and looked out. And the next morning, as soon as the sun was high enough to throw shadows into the village clearing, Danny was up and dressed. Cliff joined him a few moments later. They borrowed Jonas's boat, and it was not long until they were on their way, roaring across the placid water in the direction of the islands.

* * *

When the pile of fuel was gone and the fire was dying again, Gary took one of the heavy pieces of firewood from Ross and hit the side of the nearest gasoline drum. A loud boom reverberated through the night air.

"Why'd you do that?" Ross wanted to know.

"That's supposed to help keep grizzlies away. They don't like loud noises."

"Are you sure?"

"Well, you haven't been eaten up yet, have you?"

"You only whacked that barrel once. Here! I'll show you how to really make a noise!" He banged on the side of the half-empty gas barrel, using almost all his strength.

"You're just supposed to make a noise," Gary told him. "You're not tryin' to kill it!"

"Listen, Gary. If a little noise keeps 'em a little way from us, a lot of noise should make 'em keep their distance. As a matter of fact, I'm going to drive 'em off the island."

After a while, both boys began to tire. It was then that they decided they would take turns pounding on the gas drums. That was the way they spent the night.

The morning sun was just beginning to warm them when they heard an outboard motor and hurried down to the beach. They recognized Jonas's boat and saw that Cliff and Danny were in it.

"You guys look good!" Gary exclaimed, as the men climbed out on the beach.

"So do you," Cliff told him. "We were beginning to wonder if the bears had you for dinner last night."

"Where's your boat?" Danny asked.

Gary began to tell him the whole story of their night's adventure.

The boys got into the boat and helped pole it out into deeper water. Danny was about to start the big outboard but changed his mind and turned back to face the boys, his eyes narrowing.

"It isn't like you to take a boat without permission, Gary," he said.

The boy apologized. "We started up to the house, but then we remembered you were gone." He went on to explain about Sid and Norm coming out to steal the gas and their decision to follow them.

Danny was not surprised, but he had more questions. For one thing, he wanted to find out how they knew about the hiding place.

"It was my fault," Ross said. He wanted to tell them everything right then. He knew he would have to sometime. As Gary had said, he had to get things squared away.

But while he was trying to decide how to begin, Gary suggested they start looking for the mission boat. They soon found it on the back side of the island, pulled it up to the shore, and securely tied it by means of the anchor rope.

"Just like I thought," Gary exclaimed. "Sid and Norm *did* take our boat. But I sure didn't guess they had brought it over here and left it."

"Well, I'm glad we found it." Danny glanced at his watch. "We'd better get back to the house. We've still got some filming to do today."

As they approached the government dock about half an hour after leaving the island, they were surprised to see that the RCMP float plane was in. There were a number of people standing around it.

"I didn't know they were coming back today, did you?" Ross asked uneasily.

Gary shook his head. "I sure didn't. It looks as though they're not going to be here long, though. They're about ready to take off."

Once they were on shore, they learned the purpose of the police visit.

"They arrested Sid and Norm this morning," Del said. "They're going to take them to Pine Bluffs to stand trial for breaking and entering the Trading Post shed."

"How did they find out Sid and Norm were the ones who did it?" Gary wondered aloud.

Del explained that in their investigation, the Mounties had found pieces of the lock that had been on the shed door. Then, in the woods behind the shed, they had found an old crowbar. Acting on a hunch, they had confronted Sid and Norm with it and had told them that they were going to check for fingerprints. The boys had been so overcome by fear that they had finally broken down and confessed that they had broken into the shed.

A chill gripped Ross. His lips trembled, and for a minute or two he was sure he was going to be found out and arrested. Without bowing his head or closing his eyes he prayed silently, asking God to help him keep from being found out.

Even as he prayed, he knew God could never answer a prayer like that. He was asking God to help him hide his sin! That was probably worse than what he had done in the first place.

Trembling visibly, he changed his prayer, asking God to help him have the strength to tell the police and Danny everything that had happened.

Danny Orlis and the others had started toward the crowd of people. Ross followed them to where Sid and Norm were standing. The boys eyed him morosely but did not say anything.

The senior officer finished checking the controls of the float plane and came back to his youthful prisoners.

"I guess we're ready," he said quietly.

Ross swallowed hard and, praying once more for strength, he said, "There–there's something I'd like to tell you."

"What is it? Were you in on breaking into the shed, too?"

"No, I didn't have anything to do with that but I–I did steal some gas. That's what I wanted to tell you."

"I see."

Ross hesitated and then went on with the story. As Sid and Norm listened, their eyes rounded incredulously. "That's the most stupid thing I ever heard anybody do," Sid muttered. "You were home free. We weren't going to tell. Why didn't you leave it that way?"

"I wasn't thinking about whether you'd squeal on me or not," he continued. "I was–." The words clung to his throat, unspoken. He had not known it would be so difficult to tell anyone that he was now a Christian, that he was going to live for Jesus Christ.

"Yesterday I'd have kept still and hoped that you guys would do the same," he said. "But something happened to me last night that changed all of that. I–I became a Christian. I asked God to give me a new life. So I–I have to get things like this straightened out."

The Mountie studied him seriously but without comment. Ross did not know what would happen next. He could scarcely stand to think of being taken to Pine Bluffs and put in jail until his trial. Yet he had a good feeling. He had made things right as far as confessing was concerned. Now he would only have to pay for the gas he had stolen, and the whole matter would be taken care of.

For a short time after Ross's confession, neither of the officers spoke. At last the sergeant directed his attention to Danny. "I guess this is a matter for you to decide. How about it? Do you want to bring charges against the boy?"

"I think we'd rather handle this matter ourselves," Danny told him.

The Mountie seemed relieved.

"Actually, we don't like to make arrests," he continued. "If this boy has learned his lesson, we're glad to let you handle it."

They hustled Sid and Norm into the aircraft, climbed in themselves, and took off, heading south.

"I guess we'd better go up to the house now," Danny Orlis said quietly. "I think maybe Rene will have something for you boys to eat."

They started up the hill, but after a dozen steps or so Ross stopped and grasped Danny's sweater sleeve. "Thanks for what you did back there."

"We'll talk about it later, OK?"

"Sure," the boy replied. "I wanted to tell you the rest of what happened last night."

Danny thought he could guess, but he remained silent. Later he allowed Ross to tell him in more detail.

"Last night I finally realized that–that I was a sinner and was headed for hell." The words caught in his throat. "I've taken care of that now. I am a believer. I've confessed my sin, and things are squared away with God – I've let Him give me a new life."

Danny Orlis put his arm about the boy's shoulder, and together they walked up to the mission house.

# THE DANNY ORLIS SERIES

The Danny Orlis series, by Bernard Palmer, delivers a blend of adventure, mystery, and suspense through various settings—from the Canadian wilderness to Guatemalan jungles. Danny Orlis, an adept outdoorsman, skilled athlete, and committed Christian, employs his quick thinking, calm bravery, and biblical solutions to confront everyday problems and hair-raising dangers. Early stories focus on Danny navigating school life, sports, and outdoor challenges, while in later books, Danny and his wife Kay provide wisdom and guidance to youngsters facing lifelike situations and challenges. Having sold over two million copies, this series has made Palmer a renowned author in Christian youth literature. Palmer is also the author of the Felicia Cartright series and various other series for Christian youth.

**AVAILABLE FROM WWW.ANEKOPRESS.COM**